HONUS

HONUS

A Bastard's Childhood

Gordon Thompson

To order additional copies of this book, contact:
Xlibris Corporation
1-888-795-4274
www.Xlibris.com
Orders@Xlibris.com
42190

CONTENTS

Part Six: Religion

Part Seven: Humor

Part Eight: Tragedies

Part Nine: Departure

Dedicated to

Wilhelmina Brendemuhl

My Inspiration

And

My Wife Harriett

And

My Son Thomas

Who Made Sure I Stayed Inspired

PROLOGUE

An elderly man wandered among the gravestones in the old churchyard. The church had been rebuilt as the community had prospered, and the graveyard was now a "Memorial Garden." The entry was covered with peonies in full bloom, a rainbow of colors. The fence by the river was gone, as was the livery barn. The landscaping to the riverbank was tastefully done; gravestones edged beyond their old fenced boundaries. There were familiar names on markers: Marie Paulsen, Alice Paulsen, the Tedeman boys and their wives and some infant children. There was Elton Gunderson and Frank, Fritz, and Hans Lohmann, their families beside them. The old elm tree was gone, but Jensen's headstone inscribed with his name and dates was still there. Above them, carved on the stone, was "Rainbow Battalion" and a carefully carved Medal of Honor.

The elderly man found and paused by the Sorby plot. There was Jacob, and Mina with Lester's baby between them. Across the aisle there were Lester and Maybelle side by side. As he walked, he was joined by an aged sexton, who introduced himself as Tilman Bergson and asked if he could be of help. The visitor smiled, remembering him as one of the older boys in the preacher's confirmation class.

"Yes, as a matter of a fact you can," he said.

They walked together toward the slope of the riverbank to a spot where there was a slight indentation.

"There needs to be a marker here," he said.

The sexton shook his head, "There's no record of a grave here."

The visitor nodded, "Today there are methods to determine that without disturbing the dead; so for this grave I would like to arrange for a headstone like the one that stands over Roald Jensen's grave."

The sexton invited him into the church office to continue their discussion.

"This will have to pass the board, you know," said the sexton.

The visitor nodded, "Yes, I know." He wrote a check, handed it to the sexton along with the inscription for the stone:

This be the verse
You grave for me
Here he lies
Where he longed to be
Home is the sailor
Home from the sea
And the hunter
Home from the hill.
            R.L.S.

Above it: STUBBY MILLER, with the same medal as Jensen's carved under his name.

The sexton looked at him. "You did the stone for Jensen. You must be Honus Nelson."

The visitor smiled, "Yes, I must be."

PART ONE

The Beginning

THE LEGACY

Charles Lohmann homesteaded a quarter section on the Beavertail River some six miles southeast of Little Fork where the Beavertail joins the Red River. The valley of the Red was pure black loam, the most fertile of soil. The first years had yielded good crops. When the homestead to the south was sold, Charles was the buyer, borrowing against his own land. Piece by piece he took up land until he owned over a thousand acres. He seemed consumed by his ambition. He worked himself and his children to the very limit of endurance. Charles drove people, both by word and by example. Although a head shorter than his sons, none dared complain. Fear came first, then anger and hatred grew with their frustration.

Frank was the first to marry. He'd found a German girl who spoke only broken English. When he told his parents, his mother was pleased. Frank was quick to tell his father that he was looking for land to farm. To his surprise, Charles approved.

"You'll need a house, let's build one on the south quarter."

"I'll need land to farm before I need a house."

"The one hundred and sixty acres goes with the house, Frank. It will be deeded to you debt free."

Frank's quarter section was a choice piece of land. The house was followed by a barn, sheds and coops, then by children. Still, Frank's mixed emotions, childhood frustrations warring with adult gratitude, were never quite reconciled.

Charles did the same for Hans and Fritz when they married, giving each of the boys a running start. How much hard feeling from their childhood they took with them was difficult to say. Walfred and Cornelius never married. Charles deeded them prairie land to the east.

During Charles's lifetime his girls received no legacy. Tina went to California. Sophia lived and died in an insane asylum. Mina was banished when, unmarried, she became pregnant. Katie left home to marry, was deserted by her husband, became ill and on Mina's return was cared for by her as Charles had wished. Katie died young.

In death, to the surprise of his sons, Charles left the home farm to Tina and Mina. Later, Mina bought Tina's share of the farm and was left with the responsibility of carrying out her father's last will and testament. Though fallen from grace, Mina returned triumphant.

CHARLES LOHMANN

Charles Lohmann came to Mr. Lundeen as he had over the years when he needed credit to get next spring's crop in the ground. By now he had given each of his boys a quarter section of land with a house on it. Frank, Hans, and Fritz were married. The girls were gone.

"You still farm the whole section, Charles?" Lundeen queried.

Charles nodded.

"Your wife is in poor health?"

Another nod.

"You're no longer young, Charles, you'll need help."

"My boys will help. Fritz, Hans, Walfred, Cornelius, they'll help."

Mr. Lundeen was listening, "You didn't mention Frank."

"Frank will help," Charles said without hesitation.

"Charles, after all these years I would have no reason to deny your request. You've always made good. All of your boys except Frank have come to borrow against next year's crop. Hans and Fritz are a little on the dandy side; well-dressed and all that. Walfred and Cornelius, well, they don't really need money for what they want to do with their land. I turned them all down, Charles." He made a church steeple with his joined hands. "Charles, if your boy Frank came in here smelling like a barnyard with cow manure on his boots his credit would be good with me. He's a good farmer and a good man."

Lundeen's faint smile and final comment were, "Charles, you let me know what you need and we'll work out the terms."

Charles stood. He was stooped. His clothes fit loosely, made for a much larger man. He had passed seventy, slowing down but still fit. He would need help. His boys would help, Frank too. He knew that both Hans and Fritz had borrowed his tools and machinery, not always returning them, while Walfred and Cornelius regularly asked him for help. Still, they would all help.

Mr. Lundeen had jolted Charles as no one else could. Behind Maude in his spring buggy, dejected, deep in thought, Charles drove toward the farm. For Charles Lohmann, asking for help would be hard. Asking his boys, who would expect a return for everything they did, would be even harder. Only

Frank would help without expecting anything for it. Frank had been the first to leave home. As the oldest he had helped his father homestead, had helped clear the land while the younger children had stayed behind with their mother. Frank was the quiet, steady one, uncomplaining, undemanding to his father, who had done plenty of both. Now Frank would do it all if he asked him. Frank, the good father, the good husband, the good son, his mother's favorite, who still kept a distance between himself and his father. The reasons were a deep secret between them.

Without even a tug of the reins, Maude knew the way home. As she turned in at the mailbox, she paused for the usual mail pickup at the box. Then with quickened pace she headed toward her evening meal and rest. Charles stripped the harness and hung it in the tack room, put oats and hay in her manger, and made his way to the house.

By the time Charles had brought Maria to this land, they had been married most of twenty years, with seven living children and one in the graveyard. Two little girls came after that. Maria was a small delicate woman, with tiny hands and feet, porcelain skin, and a German ethic that made her a subservient wife who submitted to her husband's wishes and ways. After her tenth child she had been stricken with both typhoid and pneumonia. She had hovered on the edge of death during a long hot summer. Then, when hope was all but gone, she rallied. Her two grown girls, Tina and Sophie, nursed her back from exhausted skin and bones to a time at Thanksgiving when she was able to sit at table with the family. She had always been the mother-servant. Now she sat at the other end of the table from Charles. The kitchen was in the capable hands of her grown girls. It hadn't even been a dream; now it was a revelation. As she recovered, Charles came to make demands on her body. She asked, then begged, and finally rejected him. Charles left their bedroom never to return. With her mind more at ease her body began to metamorph. Her tiny body ballooned to double, then triple its size. When her heart could no longer carry the load, she died.

The undertaker did not expect what he found. He had to bring four men to wrap Maria in a tarp and carried her to the mortuary van. It was the most royal treatment that she had ever been given. Maria Lohmann, because of her huge girth, was buried in a hastily made casket and a shaped grave in which to lower it. Only two of her living children did not attend, Tina, now living in California, and Sophie, committed to the insane asylum in Farmington. Her sons, all five of them, were her pall-bearers. The sixth was Mina's husband, Jacob Sorby, who towered over the Lohmann boys as they carried the great weight to the gravesite.

Charles thanked the Ladies' Aid Society for their kindness, the food and the coffee. At the livery barn behind the church he harnessed Maude and led her out to the buggy. When he headed for home on that raw windy day, he would be alone, totally alone, for the first time in many years. As he drove toward the barn, he saw a light in the kitchen window. Leaving Maude standing harnessed to the buggy, he walked to the house where Mina met him at the door.

"Papa? Vater?" She trembled at his gaze. "I made your supper; you need to eat."

Lester was hanging on to her skirt, peeking up at the grandfather he had never seen.

"Jacob is doing the barn chores. Then we'll go."

After all the years since he had sent her away and told her never to return, Charles Lohmann was looking straight into his daughter's eyes.

"You don't need to go. Stay. There's plenty room."

Jacob called from outside, "Mr. Lohmann, I bedded and fed your horse." Then he added, "Mina, it's time we go."

Charles turned, "No, Jacob, stay. You're welcome."

It was a plea. "Please stay."

After supper Charles slumped into his platform rocker. Lester, fascinated by his great beard, approached him cautiously. Charles lifted the little boy onto his lap. Lester stroked his grandfather's beard. Together they slept.

Mina was up early. Breakfast was ready when her father appeared. He patted her back and said, "Danke schon." She smiled at him, at the pat of affection so rarely given, and the German 'thank you' so seldom heard.

Jacob came in, scraping his soles on the foot scraper and stamping them clean. "Sir, your morning chores are out of the way. Is there anything else to do?"

Charles shook his head, "You folks have your own work to do and a long way to go. I'll be going to town today."

Mina embraced her father as she left the house. He put his hand on Lester's shoulder and had said, "Goodbye, son." To Mina he said, "Auf wiedersehen, my child." There were tears in his eyes and pain behind them. Mina climbed up on the buckboard, took Lester from Jacob and bundled the two of them under a blanket. Jacob came up, took the reins and they all waved as they left the yard. As Charles became smaller and smaller as they drove away, Mina thought, "How small and thin he is."

Mina and Jacob followed the county road to Little Fork where they crossed the river into North Dakota. The Brenden farm where they worked was between Warner and Minnville. In places the road was only wagon ruts, but they had come that way and they knew the way back. It had been a long day by the time they drove into the Brenden barnyard.

Charles had watched the buckboard until it was out of sight. Then heharnessed Maude and left for Riverford. He waited at the bank to see Mr. Lundeen. They talked.

"Charles, you have enough savings for your next year's crop and then some. It's not for a banker to tell you to withdraw funds, but it's yours. You put it there."

Charles was weary. "I'll pay as I go. Get spring planting in the ground, pay my boys for their help, and hope there'll be enough left over."

Lundeen raised his eyebrows. "Enough for what?"

Charles met his eyes. "Funeral expenses," he said.

The spring planting went as planned. The Lohmanns all worked hard and Charles paid them well.

Now Charles was having trouble talking. Swallowing was an agony. His cancerous throat was choking out his life. In July he sent word for Mina to come. Frank had gotten a neighbor girl to come in and look after Charles. He could no longer talk. He wrote in his cramped hand what he wanted Mina to know. The boys had all been taken care of. They had been paid for their work. C.C. Arsgard, the lawyer, had helped Charles write his will. The funds for his burial were deposited with the Smith Brothers funeral home. "Mina, the rest is up to you," he wrote. Charles died that night.

Mina got word to Jacob to come. The Smith brothers had made the arrangements as Charles had requested. The same pall-bearers who carried Maria carried Charles to his open grave. He was a much lighter load than Maria had been. This time the boys all looked for a share of the home place.

C.C. Arsgard read the will. The boys were each mentioned in terms of what they had already received. Each had received his legacy. Each had been paid for his service since that time. Charles left the home farm to Mina and Tina. Sophie, insane, had no claim, and Mina was given the responsibility of looking out for her younger sister, Katie.

The reaction was stunned silence. Jacob Sorby did not conceal his jubilation. From a hired hand he had become a farmer, and he would farm the land they had all grown up on. He was already feeling the power of his new status. The Lohmann boys left in silence. Only Frank had turned and shook Jacob's hand to say, "Welcome to the neighborhood."

With favorable weather the last crops planted by Charles produced a bountiful harvest. It turned out to be a very good year.

Jacob went on a two-week drunken spree.

JACOB'S DEATH

Mina stood at the foot of the bed. She listened to Jacob as he rambled in and out of reality. He pulled the bedsheets into reins. He was driving a team of horses. Then he was yelling orders to the threshing crew. In a feverish moment he opened his eyes, grinned and winked, "How's my girl?" Then he was playing with Lester, scolding him affectionately as a father.

A nurse entered the room carrying a tray of pills, big ugly black ones. When she saw that Mina was there, she excused herself and turned in some confusion.

Dr. Luyben was behind her. He smiled but his voice was gruff.

"Visiting hours are over."

Mina patted Jacob's foot. "Time to go," she said as she left the room.

St. Anselm's was a three-story hospital. Jacob was on the second floor. Mina walked down the stairs to the front entrance where she paused in the afternoon sunlight. While she stood there, the nurse she had just left in Jacob's room came to her. She was very flustered and unhappy.

"The doctor asked if you would come back."

Mina started to ask why, but the nurse had turned and hurried back into the hospital. Mina climbed the stairs and turned toward Jacob's room where there were several attendants. Jacob was sitting up in bed, propped by pillows. His eyes were bulging, sightless. Jacob was dead. The doctor led her into the hallway.

"It was only a matter of time. Gangrene has no pity and there was no way to operate on such a massive wound."

Mina nodded, sighed, a deep long exhalation.

"Can you have Smith's take care of it?" she asked. Smith Brothers funeral parlor was the only one in town.

The doctor nodded. "I'll take care of it."

Once again she stood in the afternoon sunlight, dimming now toward evening. Tearless, guilty, exhilarated. "My God, how awful to feel so free." Mina's first moments as a widow were the most confused of her life.

She climbed into the old Oakland, started the motor and headed for the farm—her farm. What to tell Lester? How to pay for a funeral? Who could she ask for help? "Scratch all that," she said to herself. "Borrow the money. Help yourself." She sat up straight and drove into the farmyard.

THE ROAD

The Beavertail River meandered through the Lohmann farm. The house, the barn, and the outbuildings nestled in a sweeping bend of the river. The section road, a half-mile from the old home, went into the farm and belonged to the homestead. It was the way in and out. When Frank was deeded his quarter section to the south, he fenced along the side of the road. Turning his fence south to border his property line, he left room for a road between the fence and the line of cottonwood trees that Charles had planted for a windbreak many years before. That was where his road connected with the old road. Charles never questioned Frank's use of the road, so Frank never finished his own road.

When Charles died, Jacob Sorby had other ideas. Frank offered to grade the road and help keep it open in the winter. Jacob had told him it wasn't his to grade. It wasn't on his property. "Why don't you build your own road?" Jacob had asked. Frank saw no harm in using the road as he had been doing for so many years already and said so. It had been a good-natured argument, but it left a mark. Hans and Fritz resented it more than Frank did. "Mina owns the farm. I can't see her shutting me out," Frank had said. Still, it festered. Jacob growled to Mina, "Driving on it muddy leaves ruts. And his damn cattle leave cowshit." Mina couldn't reason with Jacob even when he was sober. The tension grew.

Mina's father had kept a small Derringer pistol in his old roll-top desk. Her alarm began when she saw Jacob fingering it at the desk. She made sure there were no shells for it. The tender truce began to unravel when Hans came to work for Frank. Deep in debt from drinking and gambling, Hans had lost his farm and left his family. So he came to Frank for help where he was a hired hand with a brother's privileges.

Jacob had come home seething because he and Hans had met in loaded wagons on the road. Hans had given way but there was barely room to pass. Hans had met Jacob's glare with a smile and a tip of his hat.

Jacob seldom drank at home, but now he did, steadily and angrily. Mina fixed his favorite meals, kept Lester away and left Jacob alone. When he came to bed late at night she heard his heavy breathing and smelled the liquor. He sweated heavily. Night sweating was not new.

Mina did the morning chores with her chore boy Lester, who helped in every way he could. Cows, pigs, and chickens were milked, slopped and fed in order. Back in the house was Jacob; unshaven, drooping eyelids and a dull glare. She poured him coffee and set Lester to filling the woodbox. She set eggs and pork belly and fresh bread before Jacob. When she turned from her kitchen chores, he was gone and his food was untouched. Mina sat down and drank his tepid coffee and ate his breakfast. When she came into the front room Jacob was sitting at the rolltop desk.

"Your brothers are going to get what's coming to them," he said.

"They've already got what's coming to them," was Mina's reply. "They've all got farms of their own. They grew up here."

Jacob sneered, "Yes, and we got the biggest one of all, and they're so jealous they'd kill for it."

Mina thought of the gun, knew it wasn't loaded, so turned away.

"There's work to do."

There were more chores: separating milk for the creamery, packing eggs. Always there was work to do, but Jacob drank the day away.

Morose and sullen, Jacob wandered around the house. Late in the afternoon he heard cattle sounds. When he looked up the road, he saw Hans herding cattle from the pasture to Frank's barn. When the cattle didn't all make the turn in the road, Frank went to head them off. At that time Jacob stormed out of the house screaming a curse at Hans.

"Get your God damned cattle off my road and off my farm or I'll kill you!"

Hans, fearful, ran to head them off. Jacob ran back into the house. When he came out again he was waving the Derringer wildly. His threats were directed at Hans and the cattle.

"I'll kill you and your God damned cattle. Every one of them, you son-of-a-bitch!"

Frank, seeing Jacob's gun, got his shotgun to come to Hans's aid. Mina had come to the window when the shouting had begun. When she saw Frank with the shotgun, she ran out on the porch screaming.

"Frank, don't shoot!"

Jacob waved the gun, pointed it at Mina. Frank fired.

Frank's long double-barrelled shotgun carried its load intact. It struck Jacob's side and left a gaping hole. Jacob lay writhing on the ground. His vital organs were all in place but he was bleeding badly. Tearfully, Lester curled himself into a pillow under Jacob's head. Frank faced Mina, eyes black with fury.

"The crazy son-of-a-bitch would have killed you."

Mina shuddered, "The gun wasn't loaded, Frank. I saw to that."

Frank's body seemed to wilt. "How could I know?" he groaned.

Mina sobbed, "You couldn't, Frank, you couldn't."

They carried Jacob into the house and laid him on a bed. Frank hurried home. He called Dr. Luyben, then the sheriff. To both he said,

"I just shot my brother-in-law. He's still alive." Mina met the doctor at the door and took him to Jacob. Dr. Luyben squinted through his rimmed glasses and shook his head. Mina had used every towel in the house to stanch the flow of blood. Jacob was quiet, barely conscious. The doctor peeled back the soggy crimson mass to see the wound.

Watching him, Mina asked, "Will he be all right?"

The doctor was reassuring, "You've done what's best for him, Mina. But best we not move him until morning to keep the bleeding down. Tomorrow we'll know."

The doctor was followed by the sheriff, who took a statement from Mina and then went to Frank's farm to arrest him. Frank opened the door for Sheriff Evenson, held out his hands.

"Cuffs?" he asked. Evenson reached for his handcuffs, paused, "Nah," and put them back.

The sheriff and Frank drove off, and an exhausted Mina lay down beside her blood-soaked husband with Lester curled up in the crook of her arm.

When the doctor arrived in the morning, Jacob was conscious; weak and pale from his blood loss. Jacob was a big man. The doctor and his burly attendants struggled to get him into the ambulance without causing more blood loss. The ten-mile ride to the hospital and the stretcher trip to the second floor re-opened the wound. Jacob was feverish and incoherent when Mina came in the afternoon.

That same afternoon Frank made bail. Four days later Jacob suddenly died. Frank was remanded. This time there was no bail.

G.J. Munson was escorted to Frank's cell. Previously he had arranged Frank's bail. Now he must visit him in jail. Munson wore a dark suit, a white shirt, and a ribbon tie.

"Permission to visit the prisoner in his cell?" he asked the deputy. When the deputy hesitated, Munson said, "Perhaps you can provide us a private place then?"

The deputy opened the door and the lawyer entered the cell. Frank looked up but said nothing. Munson produced a notepad.

"You killed a man, Frank. Let's talk."

Frank met his eyes. "Jacob was drunk. He was waving a gun around and I shot him."

"Jesus, man, you might as well plead guilty and save a trial." An exasperated Peterson slapped the pad against his thigh.

"I did kill him. I am guilty," was all that Frank said.

The mailboxes sat on each corner of the road between the two farms: Frank Lohmann to the south; Jacob Sorby to the north. The road to Frank's place and the road to the old farm was no longer a problem. Jacob was dead and Frank was in jail awaiting trial.

Mina was returning with her mail; Celia Lohmann was going to pick hers up. The two women had been friends and neighbors ever since Mina and Jacob had returned to take over the farm. Celia was a petite anonymous little woman who had borne Frank six children, four living. When still a child, she had emigrated from Germany with her family. Few people knew her by name. She was simply "Frank's wife." The awkwardness of their meeting was only momentary.

Celia said, "I'm sorry."

Mina extended her hands. They held each other. Celia said, "If I would have been there, this would never have happened."

Mina shook her head, "It has happened. We'll have to do without our men."

They talked about Frank in jail and what would happen. Celia's children were old enough to keep the farm running and Mina had always been active in running her farm. Frank was the problem. What would happen to him? Since Frank had killed Mina's husband, Celia found it hard to understand Mina's concern for him. Mina had learned that Munson was Frank's lawyer and that he couldn't get Frank to agree to any defense.

"I can't go to Mr. Munson," Mina said, "but tell Frank I would like to talk to his lawyer."

Celia went straight to Peterson. "She will be a witness for the prosecution," Munson told Celia.

"She wants to see you, Mr. Munson." Finally he agreed, "So I see her and somebody sees the both of us."

When he met with John Dortmann, the prosecutor, Munson told him of Mina's request. Dortmann had shrugged.

"The case is open and shut. If he pleads guilty the best he'll get is second degree."

Munson frowned, "What about self-defense? Sorby was drunk with a gun, after all."

"God, Munson, he shot Sorby in the back. The hard part will be finding a jury that is open-minded. Frank was a good man."

"Frank is a good man. I take it you have no objection to my visiting Mrs. Sorby?"

"None," said Dortmann.

"Fine

"Mr. Munson? Come in."

Mina was wiping her hands on her apron. Munson, wearing a dark suit, white shirt, and string tie, saw a sturdy well-built woman, mature, attractive, in her early thirties. She sent Lester off to do chores. Seated in the parlor, she brought Munson a cup of coffee.

"Cream or sugar?"

"Neither," he smiled and thanked her.

She was direct, "What is Frank going to do?" Her blue eyes locked on his. He thought, "This is a woman easy to like, easy to respect."

"Frank won't say. He says he's guilty, so why should he plead not guilty."

Mina sat forward in her chair. "This business with the road should never have happened. Frank used that road for years. Jacob wanted to show off. We had nothing until Papa willed me the farm. Jacob changed when we came here."

Munson shook his head, "Frank shot him in the back. That pretty much rules out self-defense; it doesn't leave much room for justifiable homicide either. If he's convicted of anything he goes to prison. A guilty plea would save a trial, but it's hard to know what a judge would do."

Mina was intent, "Would I have to go to court? Frank is my brother, my closest brother." Munson rubbed his chin, "Closest brother or not, he shot your husband in the back and you watched him do it. Yes, ma'am, I think you'd have to testify to that. It's the most damning testimony I know of. I'm sure you would be called." "What if I didn't?" she asked.

Munson was perplexed. "It wouldn't look very good for a wife not to testify against her husband's killer."

"Even if it was her brother?" Mina was almost whispering.

"Yes, Mrs. Sorby, even against her brother."

Mina took a deep breath. "Mr. Munson, if Frank goes to prison it will be my fault."

The lawyer was startled, "You shouldn't feel that way, Mrs. Sorby."

"Not even Frank knows what happened, Mr. Munson," said Mina.

"Then you had better tell me," he said.

Mina began, "You know that Frank didn't know that Jacob's gun wasn't loaded."

"Everybody knows that," said Munson, "I read it in the paper."

"Mr. Munson, Jacob didn't know either. I took the shells out of the gun when he went out the first time, when he told Hans he'd kill him."

Munson nodded, "That does change things, but won't keep you off the stand."

"There's more," said Mina. "I came to the door and screamed at Jacob. When he turned he pointed the gun at me. That's why his back was to Frank when he shot him."

Munson paused, "That's important, but it might not be admissible. It's only your observation. Juries are funny. What you'd be doing is testifying on behalf of Jacob's killer."

Mina's voice trembled. "I don't think Frank killed him."

"Oh?" The lawyer raised his eyebrows.

Mina told him about her visit with Jacob on the day he died. How the nurse had come in with pills just as she was leaving. How the nurse was flustered. How she was on the steps of the hospital leaving for home when she was called back. Dr. Luyben was there. He had told her that gangrene had set in and had ended Jacob's life.

"Mr. Munson, my brother Cornelius used to poison wolves when I was a little girl. I remember how they looked, stiff with staring eyes. Jacob was alive, we talked. I barely left his room when they called me back. He was propped up in bed, his eyes were staring straight ahead. It was like he was stiff, like something else was wrong. Maybe the doctor was right about the gangrene, but I don't think it had time to kill him."

Munson was stunned. The prosecutor's mother and Dr. Luyben were cousins. Dortmann would not want to deal with this. Who could blame him?

He turned to Mina, "Who knows this besides you?" he asked.

"You do."

"Nobody else, you're sure?"

"Yes," she said, "There's nobody else to tell." Munson pointed out that this was now much more complicated than how Frank pleaded his case.

He grinned, "This should cost you money, but I have no way of charging you."

When he sat down with John Dortmann, G.J. Munson, Esq. asked if they could review the situation before Frank entered his plea.

"Manslaughter if he pleads guilty, second degree if he goes to trial," said Dortmann. "Can't let a killing go unpunished," he added wryly, "Even if he's a good man."

Munson said, "Let's talk."

"Not about self defense," said Dortmann.

"Nope," replied Munson, "Justifiable homicide." Dortmann snorted, "You want me to plead your case for a judgment?"

Munson told him about Mina's role in the shooting.

"It's still manslaughter in any court," Dortmann responded.

"I was hoping we wouldn't have to go any further," said Munson.

"Where is there to go?" asked Dortmann.

Munson tossed an envelope on the desk.

"What is it?"

"It's an order to exhume Jacob Sorby's remains, signed by his widow," said Munson.

An unbelieving prosecutor asked, "For God's sake, why?"

"Because Dr. Luyben put Jacob out of his misery. 'Mercy killing' they call it. He poisoned him."

Dortmann was white, shaken, shocked, "This could ruin your reputation, Munson, and for what?"

"This could ruin your whole family, and for what?" Munson looked the prosecutor squarely in the face. He stood up, pocketed the envelope.

"The only ones who know are Dr. Luyben, Mrs. Sorby, and maybe, just maybe, the nurse in attendance at the time of Jacob Sorby's death. We'll wait for your decision before Frank Lohmann enters his plea."

To everyone's surprise, the prosecutor opted for a judgment of justifiable homicide based on incontrovertible evidence. Upon review the judgment was confirmed.

Munson saw to Frank's release.

"I hear you're a good farmer, Frank. You'd better be. This is going to cost you."

Munson never did know whether Mina had lied or not about unloading the gun or Jacob's death, but he did remove the envelope from his breast pocket. He opened it and smiled. The letter to exhume Jacob Sorby's remains was a handbill that said: "Winter is coming. Why freeze while Lange has coal?"

When Frank came home to the joy and relief of his family, he pondered with Celia about what could have made it happen. All that she could say was that Mina had asked to see his lawyer and she had seen Munson's car in Mina's yard.

Frank and the boys started grading a road out to the section road. "A road would have saved what happened," was Celia's comment. It took a couple of acres out of Frank's quarter section, but people nodded their approval. Frank wanted to make it right. Once finished, he had moved his mailbox to his own road. There was no longer a problem. Still Frank's walk back into the world was not totally simple. Frank believed in God, and "Thou Shalt Not Kill" was still the fifth commandment.

On a windy day in mid-November Frank walked on his new road to his relocated mailbox. Mina, too, was picking up her mail. Frank waved; Mina did not wave back. It was a short walk, no snow, a chill breeze from the west. She waited.

"Mina, I don't know what you did, but thank you," said Frank.

"I didn't do anything. You and Jacob were hotheads. It's over, let it be." Mina turned to walk away.

"Sis, maybe you should know some things." He turned toward the western sun. His face was bronzed from weather.

"When you and Jacob came back I hoped we could put it all away. It didn't happen. The boys in the family lived in the shadow of their father. They all hated him."

"Frank, I don't want to hear this," Mina moved away.

"Hear it and listen, Sis, you'll never hear it again, at least not from me."

Mina waited.

"You remember when Mama died? Let's start there. Tina had already gone to California. Sophia was already in the insane asylum in Fergus Falls. Did you know Tina was in a family way when she left? Remember when they locked you in the bedroom with Sophia to keep her calm? Remember she kept a butcher knife under her pillow? Didn't you wonder why? You were never afraid of her, were you? Papa had her put away. She'll never get out. I'm glad he left the old place to you, but I had warned him many years ago to leave you and Katie alone. He was a man, Mina; a man too cheap to go to a whorehouse."

"Those are terrible things to say about Papa, Frank. For what he did he can answer to God. He forgave me, Frank, for what I did wrong. If he's the man you say he was, nothing can be changed now. This was something I didn't need to know."

Mina turned and walked away. Frank watched her go. They never spoke again.

Frank was a good farmer. His boys grew into good farmers. His girls married well. Frank remained a dark and solitary man. Ten years from Jacob's death, almost to the day, he went to the machine shed. The old long-barreled shotgun was there. He put it in a vise and sawed the barrel off down to the grip. He took it to the root cellar, placed it under his chin and pulled the trigger.

TED

Barley had bearded out, headed out and turned to gold. There were over three hundred acres, half a section. Two-horse teams pulling two binders criss-crossed the field cutting a swath and spewing out the bundles of grain. 'Shocking barley takes no brains,' Ted thought. 'Stack two bundles against each other, two more on opposite sides, then six or eight more around them, that's a shock.' You think of nothing except the next two bundles. Sweat rolls off your head into your eyes and down your back. Barley beards go up pant legs, into shoes, between belt and skin, into armpits and collar. Armed with small fishhook barbs, each beard works its way until it anchors in skin. Ten acres was a day's work; Ted had done ten by noon. At dinner he ate little, but drank glass after glass of water.

From his seat on the binder Lester had watched Ted and again when they both sat at the table. He wasn't just a new hired man. He was different. Mina watched him too. Lester also saw that.

In the afternoon sun the heat and the barley beards made Ted strip to the waist. Sweat glistened off two large tattoos: on his chest a four-masted schooner, on his back a fire-spewing dragon. On his upper arms were a dagger dripping blood and a skull-and-crossbones.

By night he was beet red from the sun. He headed for the river, bathed in it, came to the table in clean clothes. Again he ate lightly; again he drank water. After supper Mina asked him if his body was burned as bad as his face. He answered with a nod. Lester had told her about the pictures on Ted's skin. He didn't know about tattoos.

To Lester's surprise, and Mina's as well, she asked the man if she could treat his sunburn. She remembered her father's way. She had Ted strip to the waist. She laid a cold towel soaked in strong tea and vinegar across his back. Then she left him to do her kitchen chores. When she returned, she repeated the treatment on his chest. With her work done, she sat by the bed. They talked.

"My name's Ted Nelson," he said. "Theodore actually, but Ted's enough."

He went on to tell her he was 'beating his way to the coast.' He called himself a merchant sailor. In Chicago he had hopped a northbound freight by mistake and ended up in Fargo.

"Glad I did now," he said.

Mina realized the compliment was meant for her. As she peeled off the towel, she looked at the ship tattoo.

"My father was the captain of the ship," he said.

"You better wear a shirt tomorrow," Mina said.

"Maybe, that barley is itchy, scratchy stuff, we'll see," he said.

The next day Ted worked just as hard and stayed covered until mid-afternoon. Again he bathed in the river before supper. Mina eyed him at the supper table.

"Heat's gone out of it," he said. "Starting to itch now."

"If you want," Mina said, "I'll do tea and vinegar again. Best to make sure."

"Sure felt good." Ted smiled.

Again they talked: he about being a boy in the Lofoten Islands, she about the farm, about Lester, about Jacob and how he died. She was more open with this stranger than she had been with anyone. When she removed the towel, she said,

"That skin is all going to peel off in a day or two."

"Do you do that too?" he asked.

She laughed at his familiarity.

"Best we wait and see."

In the field the blisters dried and shreds of skin hung loosely. Mina examined him each evening and then stretched him on the bed with a damp towel and began peeling the dead skin away. She marveled that the tattoos remained. She asked about them.

"They're part of a sailor's life," he said. "I was only a cabin boy, but they made me feel like a man."

He looked down at his four-masted schooner.

"You know the needles hurt when they go in. The pins and needles and ink can make you sick. It never did for me, but I've seen it."

Mina found the peeling skin strangely exciting. It came off in inches square from his hairless chest. As she removed a sheet she found herself looking into the intensity of his eyes. She leaned forward as though magnetized and kissed him lightly on the lips. She drew back, astonished at her own outrageous behavior. He barely smiled as he put on his shirt.

"You are quite a lady."

As the long days of harvest wore on, from shocking to threshing to open stubble-fields and straw stacks, Mina rose early each day to see to the chores, cook the meals and satisfy all needs except her own. Late one night she saw his bronze body standing beside her bed. She was amazed at his audacity, but somehow not surprised he was there. He put a finger to her lips, one to his and lay down beside her. Neither moved. When he left, he kissed her and slipped softly away into the night. Mina felt no fear of him, only a lingering curiosity. Mina had borne a child. She had known the groping of callused hands, the roughness of Jacob's demands on her body, the relief that came with his satisfaction. She had endured his frustration with his impotence when he was too drunk to carry on. Jacob had been gone for ten years. She hadn't missed him. The stirrings within her were all unanswered questions. One night she sat late on the screen porch, day's work done, quietly letting her mind wander. In the darkness of a new moon she felt that she was not alone.

"Ted?"

"Yes," came from the darkness.

He sat beside her, and they spoke in whispers for no particular reason. Mina's pulse was up. Ted was calm. These were Mina's first reflections that there was within her a person that her beating heart had known all along. They stood, walked hand in hand to Mina's room. As clothing dropped away they embraced, then lay side by side. His hands were soft, gentle, and very light. Mina's whole simmering being was responding.

He whispered, "I can take you to paradise but I can't go along."

She guessed what he meant and tried to measure her response. His hands were doing incredible things to her body. She gasped at feelings she had never known. Finally she lay in his arms in love and sleep. When she awoke, he was gone.

Over time Ted and Mina came to know this kind of love. There was little suspicion about them. Lester sensed his mother's attraction toward this man but never felt a threat.

Ted explained his impotence away as a disease from which he had never recovered. Mina craved his attention; she loved him for what he did to her; she loved him for doing it. Then one night at the height of her ecstasy there had been tumescence. She had felt it and had groped him into her body. She had felt him flowing into her, and she had simply imploded. The whole moment left Mina with a sense of wonderment, Ted with disbelief. It never happened again.

In the months that passed, Ted gained acceptance with neighbors. Even Mina's brothers and their families liked him. They accepted that Mina would want him by her side. There were those who even hinted at a union. Mina herself would see it, a future with Ted.

Arnie Busic, a Bohemian farmer, lived across the river a mile upstream. He was a big easy man with a barefoot wife who always seemed to be producing another child. His older boys farmed his land or hired out. He rarely worked himself. He also had a still. He called the product of his still "joy juice." "Yoy Yuse" from his Bohemian tongue. He turned out a powerful rotgut from barley mash. Busic's way of life did not set well with the tidy ways of the Norwegians and Germans whose farms surrounded him. They felt sorry for his wife. Most of his children's clothing were outgrown cast-offs from neighbors. Still, neighbors did come to him for bootleg. He'd fill their flat pint bottles funneled from a tin canister.

Busic liked Ted. He admired his tattoos; he said they reminded him of his Bohemian gypsy life. Slowly and slyly they became friends. Only with Ted did he share the location of his still. Only with Busic did Ted share his shipboard experience with fermentation.

Ted had been negative to tasting his product even with Busic's urging. "If I start I can't stop," he had said. Busic had left it there.

It was at Busic's place that Ted met the Swanson brothers, Teddy and Olaf. They were free-wheelers from Riverford, looking for money without earning it. They came to Busic, bought in quantity, paid cash. They were loud, brash, confident, and clearly on the take. Teddy Swanson had worked in the warehouse by the railroad tracks in Riverford. Heisting a warehouse at night and loading a truck with potato bug killer, paris green, was his plan. Selling it to farmers off-season would save the farmers money and conceal the theft. Ted listened. They asked him in.

"Here, let's drink on it," they said.

Ted was negative to that.

"Can't trust a man who won't drink with you," was all Teddy said.

Ted drank.

When Mina saw him arm-in-arm with the Swansons, weaving their way down the road, everything changed. With their intimacy gone, Mina filled every waking moment with work. There were strange stirrings and changes in her body. She had borne Lester in her twenties. Now in her forties she came to realize another child was on the way, all from that fleeting moment with Ted. She ignored the first whispers, but when she saw the hurt in Lester's eyes, she sat with him and explained, not how or why, but simply that there was a child in her just as he had been. For the rest, Lester didn't ask, she didn't tell.

Now Ted was spending his time with the Swanson brothers. The theft had gone undetected. A farmer, Ollis Pearson, had fixed a hiding place. At the price they asked, selling the Paris Green was easy.

Jaunty and smart after drinking with the Swansons, Ted was wearing new clothes when he came to see Mina. When he saw her, he was thunderstruck. Mina's level gaze shattered him.

"I've ruined you," he moaned. "What can we do?"

"We," and she emphasized the "We," "have started a life. I'm going to have a child even though I'm too old, even if it's shameful. This is my land. I will live on it and work it. If you want to have any say about this baby, it's up to you. Right now you're in bad company. Remember that."

The honking horn reminded Ted that the Swansons were waiting.

"I'll be back," Ted said as he turned from Mina.

When he told the Swansons, they were gleeful.

"Gawd, you lucky bastard. Now you can be a farmer; do what you want. You'll be giving the orders."

Ted sobered them, "I want out of this stuff we're doing; this baby changes everything."

They didn't think so. "We're all in it. We hang together. No way to back out now."

That night Ted caught the southbound freight for Chicago. Soon the whole plan unraveled. Ollie Pearson turned informer, showing the sheriff where the paris green was hidden. The Swanson brothers were arrested. A fugitive arrest warrant was issued for Theodore Nelson. The Daily News carried the story. That was how Mina found out. She hadn't bought any paris green, but those who had were sternly warned to turn it in.

Ollie Pearson was dismissed for providing state's evidence. The Swanson boys pleaded guilty and each got six months in county jail. The fugitive warrant was for grand larceny. Ted was labeled the ringleader of the thieves.

The letter to Mina came postmarked from San Francisco. In it, Ted asked Mina to forgive him and to give the baby his name. His strangest request was, if it was a boy, would she name him Honus, after the great baseball player Honus Wagner. He did not know, nor could she tell him, that he would be arrested if he ever showed his face in Riverford.

Mina struggled through the next two months of averted eyes, cruel gossip, pitiless snubs, glares. Hardest of all was the pity that came from those whom she had trusted. She thought of Lester, the loyal one, who went silently about his work with never a word of blame. What if the baby was crippled? What if she died in childbirth? There was no stopping. She had been alone before, but never like this.

Mrs. Nottsly had been midwife to many births. Her task with Mina was an easy one. She arrived in the morning. By noon the baby was born, bathed, swaddled and lying peacefully by his mother; a boy, whole and healthy. He was given his father's name. Reluctantly, Mina granted Ted's request. Honus Nelson was living his first day on the planet.

Letters came from faraway places: Hong Kong, Shanghai, Calcutta, Genoa, London. Mostly they repeated that he had shipped out of San Francisco or New York and told of storms at sea.

"I'm all right, but I miss you," was the closing of each letter.

Two years passed. The boy had toddled his way into Mina's heart and Lester's too. On the day Ted came, Honus was sitting on the steps. Wide-eyed, he watched the stranger approach. Ted reached out a hand. The boy took one finger. No word was spoken. When Mina saw him, she said, "Oh Ted." They talked and she quickly told him what had happened. It mattered little. He had been seen in town. The sheriff knew where to look. By night he was a prisoner. Arraigned, he pleaded guilty. He was a fugitive outlaw who had sired a child out of wedlock, so the court showed no mercy. He was remanded to the State Prison in Stillwater with a sentence of three years. Mina had taken the boy to see him before he was taken away and was allowed into his cell with a trustee attending. Ted was thin and pale. He and Mina talked, but Ted never took his eyes off the boy.

"He has my name and he's my next of kin. It's in the records, Mina, he's my next of kin."

Mina choked back tears. "Write," she said, "Now we know where you are. We'll write back."

In the months that followed there were letters, not many. First he worked in the kitchen. Then he had been taken off work details. Then he was in the infirmary. After nearly a year, a letter came with the official return from the prison warden. It was addressed to Honus Nelson, next of kin:

> We regret to inform you that your father died this date. The cause of death was advanced tuberculosis. Please confirm with us your plans for interment, etc."

A tearful Mina sat down with her boys, uncomprehending Honus, silent Lester.

"We'll have to bring him back and bury him here," she said to Lester. "I know how you must feel, but please go with me and Honus to get him."

Lester never said a word, but he went.

When they arrived in Stillwater, the letter was their access to the outer office of the gray prison. The uniformed man who spoke to them seemed agitated and went to speak with his superior. Together they came to ask,

"Who is Honus?"

Mina pointed wordlessly at her little boy. The officers were red-faced and apologetic.

"His body was claimed at the time of his death."

"But who?" asked Mina.

"His wife, she was with him when he died."

Mina stood, silent. Then she asked, "Why send this little boy the letter?"

"He was listed as next of kin, but the letter should never have gone out."

"What was her name? Who was she? Where did she take him?"

"It's confidential. We can't divulge that information."

Mina spoke loudly enough to be heard throughout the office, "You can't even tell his own son where he was taken?"

The two men looked at each other. One said, "San Francisco."

PART TWO

The Molders

STUBBY

Mina and Honus had gone to town for groceries. Chester Swenson, the grocer, had helped them load the trunk and part of the back seat. The old Oakland motor car looked like a grocery box on wheels, great disk wheels with small hard tires. They crossed the bridge going out of town and were passing Charley Peterson's truck farm when they saw him, a small man by the side of the road. The boy, barely big enough to look over the dashboard, watched Mina slow down as they approached. She stopped, leaned across the boy and cranked down the window.

"Looking for work?" she asked.

The man's grin was tentative.

"Harvest work, a dollar a day and your keep."

What he had was in a knotted bandanna. He hesitated.

"If you want to come along, climb in."

Hesitation gone, he opened the back door and crowded in with the groceries.

"We're just starting threshing," she said. "At least two weeks work if it doesn't rain."

She had sized him up: short, very short, heavyset, red curly hair, lots of it, blue eyes in a ruddy face.

"My name is Miller, ma'am. People call me Stubby."

"I'm Mina Sorby," she said. "My farm's about ten miles north of town. Ready to start harvest. Wheat first, then barley and oats. Ever shock grain?" she asked. The boy was peering over the seat at Stubby.

"Yes, ma'am," he said, "but not a lot."

He gave Honus a huge wink that retreated the boy back in his seat. They stopped at the mailbox. Mina got out and picked it out of the mailbox, examining it as she got back in the car. The Daily News and a couple of letters. The last mile of road led to the farm house. When she stopped, Stubby Miller asked her where she wanted the groceries. She walked ahead and showed him the kitchen table. He made four trips to bring in all the groceries. She noticed that he gave the boy small packages that he could carry and watched that he got it done. When he finished, Mina handed him a glass of water and thanked him.

"Your boy did a big part, you know," he said.

She smiled and agreed. She pointed to a low building between the house and the barn.

"That's the bunkhouse, there's bedding and whatever you need. Minnick is the foreman. He'll be in for supper. I better get it started."

Stubby turned to leave and picked up his knotted bandanna. He opened the door, turned and gave another huge wink to the watching boy who smiled, just barely. Stubby turned and walked toward the bunkhouse.

MINNICK

A thundershower during the night had benched the threshing crew. By noon the sun was out, so it would be dry enough for the harvest tomorrow. Most of the men were sitting or stretched out on benches outside the blacksmith shop. There was some talk but not a lot. They chewed on straw, occasionally broke wind, laughed. Minnick was the straw boss, a towering big surly Irishman. This enforced idleness made him even surlier than usual. He was rawboned, heavy-handed, very much the boss man. His big hands and sinewy muscles told of winters in the north woods as a lumberjack. The crew took his orders without question and behaved pretty much as he behaved. They watched him and did what they thought he wanted. He had been around since a time before Mina was a widow. He and Jacob had gotten drunk and cracked some heads around Fargo and Riverford; shared a jail cell on few occasions. With Jacob gone it was only natural Minnick should think about his chances with Mina.

Now she was running the farm. There was money in the bank and the prospect of another good year. Minnick was a good man; good at what he did and Lester followed him around as if he were God. Minnick liked Lester and taught him about machinery and farm work. Lester was seventeen, a man-sized boy and eager to learn. Mina knew all that; yet Minnick was a tie to the past that she wanted no part of.

Mina was working in the kitchen peeling potatoes, washing muddy carrots, getting ready to feed the threshing crew. Men who hadn't worked all day would still be hungry when they came to the table. Honus had pulled the carrots for her and had helped dig the potatoes. There would be field corn, pork chops and a raisin cake, all for men who hadn't done a lick of work all day.

Stubby had kept to himself that day, apart from the crew. Up in the haymow he had dozed and watched a flock of pigeons in their mating game. When he came out of the barn he looked toward the house, saw the boy in the window and waved. The boy waved back and laughed. There were mud puddles dotting the yard from the barn to the house and beyond to the blacksmith shop. Stubby began a slow ballet around each puddle. With his long arms and short legs, he had the ungainly grace of a monkey. He could spring high in the air across larger puddles. Through the window Mina smiled and shook her head. The boy laughed uproariously. Minnick, watching from the blacksmith shop, glowered.

"I hate that little son-of-a-bitch," he muttered.

Stubby was doing a muddy pirouette when Minnick clambered to his feet. In great strides he crossed the yard, ignoring the puddles, splashing through them. When he reached Stubby he grabbed the front of his bib overalls.

"You silly-assed little cocksucker. I've had enough of you."

Through the window the boy watched horrified. Mina's face was taut. Minnick lifted the little man off the ground. Stubby went completely limp. Minnick lifted him to his own eye level. Stubby's body was limp, a dead weight. The big man thrust his head toward Stubby's upturned face. He started to spit into Stubby's face. What happened then was so sudden that cause and effect were one. The limp body became a steel spring. Stubby's head struck Minnick squarely in the nose. His knees came up into the big man's groin. Minnick staggered. He loosened his grip and Stubby wriggled free. The boy in the window choked a scream back to whisper, "Run, Stubby, run!"

Stubby did not run. He backed off, then rammed Minnick off balance. He dropped to his knee, grabbed Minnick's heel with one hand and his knee with the other. The big man fell full length on his back into a puddle, landing with a bone bruising thump that vibrated across the yard. Stubby stood up and looked down at Minnick, who stirred, opened his bloodshot eyes, raised himself up on one elbow, then the other. Dazed but still uttering that guttural snarling growl. Stubby stepped to one side to walk past Minnick. Minnick moved to sit upright. As Stubby passed Minnick, he swung the heel of his right hand to Minnick's forehead. The skin and bone contact cracked like a rifle shot. Minnick's head splattered muck in every direction. This time he made no effort to get up.

Mina and the boy had watched in amazement. They watched, still amazed, as Stubby walked to the bunkhouse. He was crying. Great shoulder-shaking sobs.

Minnick was all right except for a pulpy, bulby nose, a stiff neck and some very tender gonads. He cleaned himself up and made his way to the house. Stubby was already there, his rucksack packed and tied. He had already told Mina and the boy that it was best that he leave.

When Minnick arrived, Lester was with him. He got straight to the point. "Mina, this man's got to go. He's been trouble ever since you hired him."

Mina looked at Stubby, "He called you a cocksucker, Stubby. Are you?"

Stubby stiffened, his face reddened. Minnick sneered. Mina turned to Honus.

"I don't think you should hear this talk. Go away."

Stubby took a deep breath. "Ma'am," he said, "I've had to do some things in my life that I'm not proud of, but there's no man on this farm who can say that about me. It's not true."

Mina looked at Minnick. "Well?"

Minnick smirked, "Do you believe that?" He glared at Stubby. "He even breeds with the sheep out there in the shed."

The boy had left the room; out of sight but not out of earshot. Now he returned. Stubby was red with shame and embarrassment. The boy had tears in his eyes.

"You do too, Mr. Minnick. I saw you, and I saw you show Lester how to do it too."

Minnick stood as though rooted to the floor. Lester turned beet-red. Mina looked from one to the other and back. There was no room for denial. Minnick was hoisted on his own petard.

"Minnick, I've seen enough and heard enough today. I'll pay you through the end of the week, but I want you off the place tonight. Minnick looked at Lester, who looked away. He glared at the boy.

"Who's going to run the rig for you, Mina? You'll lose your crop."

Mina's eyes had an icy blue quality when she answered.

"Well, you're not going to. I hope Lester can. Seems like you've taught him things. If he can't, I'll do it myself."

Lester, elated with his promotion, avoided Minnick and never spoke. Minnick walked away that afternoon. Years later someone said he had married a widow and had a farm in Illinois.

Mina asked Stubby if he wanted to stay. If he wanted to, he could. The boy's eyes pleaded. Stubby stayed.

The next day was dry enough to thresh. At the breakfast table Mina had told the hired men that Lester would be running the machinery. She didn't say he was boss or that he was in charge. Lester knew every Zirc fitting and every spot of moving parts that needed oiling. He did what he knew and nobody said a word. The hayracks were bundled to the top and headed in by the time Lester fired up the Allis Chalmers and put the power take-off in gear. The tractor pulley slowly worked up to speed and the great maw of the separator with its flashing dragon's teeth was ready to slash into the oncoming bundles of grain. Stubby took his spot under the conveyor, ready to spike pitch the bundles that missed the conveyor. The two men on the rack jumped to the ground. They came over to Stubby. They towered over him. One grinned.

"How about trading jobs for a while?" The other one jerked his head toward the rack, "How about working with me?"

Stubby grinned too, "Sure, why not?"

Minnick had put a short man to do a tall man's job. The crew themselves knew it and made it right.

By mid-morning the heat was on them. Blazing sun, chaff, dust, and straining muscles. The boy and Mina came to the field pulling a wagon with a five-gallon creamery can of cold nectar, a tray of cookies, and leftover raisin cake. As the racks emptied, the men stopped off and emptied the cups of nectar, leaned in the shade of their racks and ate their treats. After the cookies and cake were gone, the nectar can lighter, Mina and the boy pulled the wagon back toward the house. They stopped by a patch of corn and filled the wagon with enough for supper.

For supper there were great bowls of boiled new potatoes, platters of pork chops, gravy, garden vegetables along with the corn, and fresh rhubarb pie. There was a great pitcher of water at each end of the table. After work the men washed up in basins by the bunkhouse. Stripped to the waist they snorted into the water like great walruses, dried on common towels, dressed and waited for a supper signal from Mina. Among threshing crews Mina had the reputation of being a good cook.

When the supper signal came there was no delay. They moved into the dining room. Chairs scraped into place. Mina waited on the table. The men were polite in the way that hungry men are polite. They made sure they kept the serving dishes moving. Everybody ate heartily because there was plenty. The main order of business was eating so there wasn't much talk. Supper over, everyone mumbled thanks to Mina and left the house. Outside some rolled smokes and sat smoking by the bunkhouse. Others stretched out on the benches by the blacksmith shop relishing the luxury of rest and a full stomach.

When Lester came in, Mina had the end of the table cleared. He had washed up, had that scrubbed look about him. He must have seen the proud look in her eyes because he smiled.

"I can do it, Mamma, today was all right."

She brought him his supper. "I knew you could, Lester, you did just fine."

Supper over, Honus sat on the front porch in the evening light. Darkness waits longer in the northern summer. As twilight dimmed, burning straw piles dotted the fields between the farm and the Red River a few miles away.

Honus was sitting with his knees drawn under his chin. The silence was marred by one lone mosquito who made a landing on the boy's leg and lost its life. Stubby appeared out of the darkness chewing a stem of quack grass. Wordless, he sat on the bottom stair of the porch. Under the shelter of the stairs and the porch, Honus's dog Jube stirred. Eventually the boy spoke.

"Why were you crying after you put Minnick down?"

Stubby chewed on his grass stem for a minute before he answered.

"I guess I never wanted to hurt anybody, and I knew I hurt him."

Honus swallowed hard. "He could have killed you. Mamma said so."

Stubby tossed away the grass stem, "But he didn't, did he?

Almost in a whisper the boy said, "I was so scared just watching. Weren't you scared?"

Stubby grinned, "Shitless, scared shitless."

He held up his clenched hand. "You see where your thumb and finger curl together? Well, there's a muscle in your ass that works like this." He squeezed his fist several times. "When your asshole starts doing that, you're scared. And my old turd cutter was going a mile a minute, believe me." They both laughed.

"As for killing me, Sunshine, maybe I've lived too long already."

Those words would haunt the boy the rest of his life. Honus yawned.

"Time to hit the hay, buddy, tomorrow is on its way," said Stubby as he headed for the bunkhouse.

ELTON GUNDERSON

Elton Gunderson was a big pear-shaped man. He usually showed up when the threshing crews were laid up by wet weather. There was little to do. Some stretched out on benches, or whittled, or just sat. Nobody liked Elton much, but he was a talker, better than nothing. He had a string of off-color jokes. As he got warmed up, his jokes went from dirty to filthy.

Mina didn't like the man. She couldn't very well run him off, but she stayed away from him when he came around. She felt sorry for his childless wife who did both housework and field work for her lazy husband.

It had rained the day before but today was a clear day with the sun shining and a good breeze: drying weather. Elton came by in his one-horse buggy. He climbed down, chewing on a stem of quack grass. The first talk was about weather. Weather was never as good as it needed to be. He began his storytelling with something like, "Have you heard what Rastus did to Daisy?" or "What happened when Jacob married Inga?" He had a string of traveling salesman jokes as well as hired man jokes. He got going with little encouragement. A chuckle or even a grin would get him started.

Honus and Stubby were sitting on a bench with the men. Stubby was showing the boy how to cut a willow whistle, working the bark loose, slotting it just right and shaving one edge.

Elton laughed at his own jokes; he didn't pay much attention to anyone in particular. Some of the men looked sideways at the boy sitting with them and listening to this kind of talk.

Elton wore bib overalls that bulged over his stomach. He dug his hands down inside the bib while he talked. Stubby was listening as he cut the whistle. He was irritated by Elton's storytelling in front of the boy. Honus was not paying any attention to Elton or the men. When Stubby finished the whistle, he handed it to the boy. Glancing at Nelson, he said in a low voice,

"I wonder what he's doing with his hands."

Honus blew the whistle. It was a good one that cut into the middle of Elton's story.

"Go somewhere else and blow your God damned whistle."

No one spoke.

Honus stood, "I'm sorry, Mr. Gunderson." He turned to leave then turned back.

"Mr. Gunderson, what do you do with your hands in your overalls?"

Everybody laughed, big belly laughs. Gunderson turned beet red and started to say something about a snot-nosed little ba . . . Thought better of it when he saw Lester. Climbed into his buggy and left.

When Lester told Mina what had happened, she told him that she would give the boy a talking to. He had no business talking that way. To herself she said, "I wish I had had the nerve to say it."

LESTER

Lester began his life on a farm in North Dakota. His father, Jacob, was the strawboss and his mother, Mina, was the cook. Mina described him as looking starved when he was born. She told people that you could see his ribs, and his forehead and temples were all sunken in. Still, he weighed over ten pounds. From the time he could walk he wanted to help. Mina called him "Chore-boy." In a homemade wagon he hauled stove wood, buckets of water. Whatever she asked him to do, he did.

Everything was serious to Lester. Big and rawboned, he had the build of a man by age ten. He had a shambling gait that resulted from knock knees and pigeon toes. Painfully, he began to read in school. Years later his problem would have been diagnosed as dyslexia. Yet he could do arithmetic very effectively. He worked hard in school, struggling with both reading and writing. Teachers saw his effort and helped him because he was so serious. As he grew he became a help to teachers, always there if a pupil challenged. Never a bully, he seemed able to persuade his peers and still be friends. It was no surprise when he reached the eighth grade in the little country school that the examinations would be a tremendous hurdle. The teacher somehow got permission to give him his examination alone. The county examiner allowed it and made him an exception. When he passed on a Friday afternoon he went home, did the evening chores and was back in the field on Saturday morning.

Lester was focused. Farming was always his life. Jacob had died when Lester was still a small boy. From that time on, Mina ran the farm. She knew how to take advice. She knew how to use that advice to make money. Painful as it was for him, Lester read magazines such as "The Successful Farmer." The ideas were there and Lester was restless to try them. Mina listened, even read the thumbworn magazines, but found no time for innovation. Finally Lester convinced her to try raising onions on a five acre patch.

"You plant, you cultivate, you weed, you spray, you harvest, you sell," she told him. "And you do it all while we all work."

In other words, the onion project was tacked on to working a 640 acre section of land.

Lester kept his records: cost of seed, special planting, thinning, weeding. He had to hire help for thinning and weeding. Mina smiled a little tightly when she advanced him the money to pay his help. The field where potatoes had been the usual crop looked strange with its green sprouts popping up. The weather was kind and come August the stems began to dry and it was time to harvest. Mina's potato broker agreed to market the onions, but first the onions had to be picked and packed in net bags instead of the burlap bags that were used for potatoes. Tight-lipped, Mina advanced Lester the money to buy the sacks.

Harvesting onions involves sorting. Dry stems were marketable. Wet stems, bottle-necks, were discarded because they rot. When the boxcars were loaded and routed, Lester drove the empty Reo Speedwagon truck into the yard. He went into the house and sat down at the old rolltop desk. After he worked out his balance sheet, he showed Mina the figures and the check. His expenses left almost a thousand dollars profit.

"It's yours, Lester. It was a lot of hard work. You earned it."

"It only took up five acres, Mama. That's two hundred dollars an acre," Lester said. He felt proud.

Mina said, "You have all those onions that didn't sell. Are you just going to let them rot in the field?"

Lester thought about that. "We'll truck them over to the cow pasture. No point in letting them go to waste."

So a truckload dumped in the pasture and the cattle ate them eagerly. However, the catch came the next day when the cows were milked. Onion-flavored milk was separated into onion-flavored cream, which became onion-flavored butter. Mina grimly used it all.

"Lester, you made money, but you sure don't know your onions."

The next spring Lester sat down with Mina at the kitchen table. He had worked out a plan to put the same five acres into sunflowers and to raise chickens. Mina expressed her exasperation.

"Why don't you put in onions again? You had a good paying crop."

Lester's answer was even more exasperating. "I did that. I know that I can." He sat there at the table folding and unfolding his big farmer-boy hands.

Mina shook her head, "It's your money if you want to risk it."

Lester put his elbow on the table and his head in his hand. "It may take more than what I got, Mama. Will you back me if it does?"

"How much more?"

"Maybe five hundred."

"Maybe nothing! I want facts and figures," Mina left no room for argument.

Lester researched the Sears Roebuck Catalogue for prices: brooder pens, feeders, wire net; then he went to town to price chicken feed and live chicks. He came home sober and wiser. Instead of a thousand chicks there would be five hundred. Old Osbert Lange liked him, offered him credit on the chicken feed and sent him off in the direction of some used brooder pens.

When Lester sat down with his mother this time, he had his arithmetic done. He told his mother he could do it on his own, except for one thing, the price of sunflower seeds at planting time.

"It's a new crop around here; nobody knows for sure what seed will cost."

"Or how to plant it or how to cultivate it or anything," Mina added.

"I do," was all Lester said, pointing to a thumbworn copy of "The Successful Farmer."

"And what do you plan to do with all those chickens?" asked Mina.

"Castrate 'em," Lester grinned.

Mina sat back in her chair thunderstruck. "God, boy, what are you getting yourself into?"

"It's called caponizing, Mama, like you change a bull to a steer."

Mina shook her head. "For all the chickens I've cleaned, I have yet to see one with nuts hanging loose."

Lester laughed. "What you do is you make a little slit alongside the backbone just above the leg joint. There's a little oyster that's attached in there, and you pull it out with a tool called a forcep. Then you do the same thing on the other side of the backbone. Then you got a capon instead of a chicken."

Mina was listening. "So what happens then?"

"Well, they grow faster and bigger. They put on more meat that's more tender. Big city restaurants pay twice what they pay for chicken."

Mina was skeptical, "I can't see a chicken just standing there and letting you do that to him."

Lester wrinkled up a little on that. "Well, there's a thing called a spreader. You tie the wings back and the legs—it's shaped like a bow." He drew a picture showing how it worked.

Mina's comment was, "Who's going to do that? Looks to me like it takes four hands."

Lester hesitated, "Maybe Honus would."

"There you go with your maybe again. You'd better find out from him," Mina said, knowing full well that the boy would do anything Lester asked.

Mina kept firing questions at Lester. It dawned on him that she wanted him to succeed and this was her way to help him.

Lester got his brooder pens set up inside the shelter of the machine shed, feeders ready to go and waiting for chicks. When they arrived in late March, the weather behaved. There was no heat in the machine shed. None was needed. Lester gulped at the thought. He was lucky. He lost a few chicks, but he watched them carefully. Voracious, they seemed to eat their weight every day. They were a breed called White Giants. As weeks passed they feathered out into pullets and approached their puberty.

Lester was nervous as he organized his caponizing task. He divided the brooder area so that after the operation the capons would be segregated. Lester caught the first bird, showed the boy how to tie it down, then he performed the operation. It was very important to be thorough when reaching in with the forceps. The whole teste had to be cleanly removed or else the pullet would develop into a strange gargantuan creature with exaggerated sex characteristics, huge comb and wattle, legs and feet out of proportion to the rest of the body. These poor creatures were called "slips." They became distinguishable within a month as they were looking for a fight and behaving like roosters. Several of the operations resulted in broken blood vessels, internal bleeding and death for the pullet.

Lester and the boy worked through the day until they no longer had enough light. The second day ended with most of the chickens caponized. And the third day was matter of catching the rest, for now the pen was nearly empty and the birds could be elusive.

Lester's experimental chicken project attracted neighborhood interest but no copiers. Too much work—too risky.

Osbert Lange mixed Lester's chicken feed to his own formula. Then he took it a step further and told Lester to buy a liquid nicotine compound and mix it with the feed. The nicotine came in five gallon cans with the skull and crossbones clearly on the label. The right amount created a continuous appetite. An overdose was deadly. Lester did his measuring to the last drop. The growth was phenomenal. Old Osbert had extended Lester credit on the feed; now he came back into the picture to advise Lester about selling. The weight of the birds was eight to ten pounds. On Osbert's advice, Lester crated up his birds and sold them live weight to the packing house in West Fargo. After paying Osbert he was still well ahead of his expenses.

The sunflowers were a spectacular crop, taller than corn with huge heads that seemed to follow the rays of the sun. Hail could ruin a crop in minutes; wind could flatten it beyond repair. But it didn't hail and the wind didn't whip. Lester was lucky, as there was a market for sunflower seeds in the Twin Cities at General Mills. Again Lester made a profit.

That fall Lester went to town, bought himself a new suit, a hat, an overcoat. The suit had to be altered to fit his big frame. When he came back for the last fitting, he wore it out the door. He went down to Eric Torgesen's photo studio and sat for a portrait, coat, hat and all. Lester was two months short of his twentieth birthday. He had proved himself. He was a good farmer.

PART THREE

Education

THE WATKINS MAN

The section road was built up high by the earth of the drainage ditch dug next to it. It was a dirt road that rutted when it rained and trailed a cloud of dust when it was dry. A car could be seen a mile away and there was still half a mile to the farmhouse when a car got to the mailbox. On a late afternoon, Albert "Bertie" Black turned at the half-mile road to the farmhouse. He drove a Model A Ford Cabriolet with an oversize trunk attached to the back. When he parked in the farm yard, he took out a display case and headed for the house. Mina was a regular customer. She had told him that his black pepper, cinnamon and other spices were better than those in the store. She always bought the nectar extracts that working men liked to drink mid-morning in the fields. Mina came out of the kitchen to meet Bertie. He was a small man of slight build, always with coat and tie, and a bowler hat. He was English. He tipped his hat,

"Mrs. Sod-a-bee, how aww you?"

She, as always, smiled at his accent and confirmed her wellness. Honus looked on while he opened his display case to show his wares. She made her selections quickly, sure from experience what she wanted.

Bertie Black would never admit to being a peddler. Watkins salesman, yes. His territory was the whole of Black Loam County. Door to door, house to house, farm to farm. He was well known, liked, and occasionally snickered at for his accent and the clothes he wore. Nobody knew any more about him than that.

When Bertie returned from the car with Mina's order he gave the boy a package of Black Jack licorice chewing gum. That got a big smile from both giver and receiver, and a thank you from both the boy and Mina. Also tucked under his arm was the biggest book the boy had ever seen.

"Ma'am, I would like to show you this book. It's called *Circle of Knowledge, a Compendium of Essential Information*. It's like a whole library all in one book. Your boy is probably a little too young to read from it just yet, but it will sure answer a lot of his questions when he goes to school."

Honus had opened the book to Astronomy. His eyes were squinted from concentration. Then he read aloud,

"Our Planetary System: any heavenly body that shines by reflected sunlight and revolves about the sun. The major planets in their order from the sun are Mercury, Venus, Earth, Mars, Jupiter, Saturn, Uranus, and Neptune." Honus looked up and grinned. Bertie Black swallowed,

"Maybe he's not too young after all. How old are you, son?"

Mina answered for him, "He's seven, but he's always been able to read."

The price of the book was ten dollars. The Watkins man did not press when Mina said, "We can't afford it."

The boy shook his head in crestfallen agreement with his mother. Bertie Black closed the book and turned to leave.

"Quite a lad you have there, ma'am." And he tipped his hat.

Honus watched him, book tucked under his arm as he walked to the car. Then he turned and went into the kitchen.

Mina was standing over the stove. There were tears in her eyes. The boy leaned his head against her hip. Mina reached for the old Monarch Coffee can above the stove, opened it and took out a ten dollar bill.

"Sicum. You can still catch him," she said as she handed Honus the money.

Black's car had a self-starter so he was ready to move, engine running, when he saw the boy waving, yelling "Wait," as he ran barefoot across the yard."

"The money," he panted, "Mama changed her mind."

"Your mama is a very smart woman, must be where you get it from."

He left the car running, opened the trunk and handed the book down to Honus.

"It's heavy. Can you carry it? Seventeen hundred and twenty-three pages of fine print. Read every word, son."

The boy could and he did.

THE CRYSTAL SET

Lester had seen it in an ad in 'The Successful Farmer' magazine. "Entertaining, Enlightening, a Window on the World," the ad had read. Lester sent away for it. It came in a small packing box marked "Fragile." There were a pair of earphones, a loop aerial, a battery, a filament and a small round silvery crystal tube. Once assembled, the earphones could be plugged into it and you had a crystal set.

Lester lost interest almost immediately because the earphones were too small for his head size. Also, he found out about radio. Atwater-Kent had put to market a battery operated machine shaped like a church steeple. It came equipped with a switch, a dial, and an aerial.

When the radio came, Honus asked if he could try the crystal set. Lester told him, "Keep it. It's no good." The earphones really appealed to Honus. On him they fit. It was a thrill to hear a voice or music coming through them. Much to Mina's aggravation they also cut out outside sounds like "Dinnertime" or "Time for bed." The local station was WDAY in Fargo. Every afternoon after school there was "Little Orphan Annie," where an Ovaltine shaker would be sent for three foil seals; "Dick Tracy" and his decoder ring; "One Man's Family" with Father Barbour and his bewildering offspring, boxing with Joe Louis starting his career, even the heartbreaker football game in a snowstorm where Northwestern beat Minnesota for the national championship. The crystal set was magic and it didn't need to be shared. For Honus, the crystal set and *The Circle of Knowledge* were the bridge to a larger world.

Honus listened uncomprehending to the deepening crisis called the Depression. Mina listened grimly, with Lester, to the same news on the Atwater-Kent. Banks closed, money was lost, prices dropped to pennies on the dollar. Farmers traded with produce; wheat for flour, eggs for overalls. A hundred pound sack of potatoes got a dollar's worth of groceries. Canning and curing were part of life on the farm. "Make do" was the password for survival. Farmers in debt lost their homes, packed up and headed west, much as the pioneers of an earlier century had done.

Honus had read in his *Circle of Knowledge* that food, shelter, and clothing were basic to life. No one under Mina's roof went unfed, unsheltered or unclothed. They thrived, but only somewhat prospered.

THE FIRST DAY

The church and the school house faced each other across the county road. The diggings from the drainage ditch made it a high road. The school yard was the corner of young Fritz Lohmann's quarter section. Charles Lohmann had dedicated the school yard to the county long before he deeded the land to his son. Indeed, young Fritz had his schooling there. After him there had been Sophie, Cornelius, Walfred, Mina, and Katie. The same school still served when Mina brought Honus to the school house on his sixth birthday. School started at age six whenever the birthday happened. For Honus, it was the eleventh of March.

Mina brought Honus to the door. Heads turned in their direction as Miss Foster, the teacher, came to meet them. The women greeted each other and Honus was directed to a seat. Then Mina was gone. Clutching his lunch pail in one hand and a pencil and tablet in the other, Honus sat down at a desk. Desks were attached one to the other by cast iron grill work. Each had a wooden top with a dry inkwell in the corner, and a shelf underneath. The teacher saw that every one had work before she came back to him. Unsmiling, she asked him to hang his coat in the cloakroom. There were no introductions. When Miss Foster got back to Honus, she was carrying a reader, an arithmetic book, and a Palmer handwriting manual.

"You keep these things in your desk, and when I call on you, I will tell you what to do," she said.

Honus was being watched by another boy his age who was laboring over the alphabet in his handwriting manual. There were older boys dressed in bib overalls and flannel shirts and older girls in gingham dresses. They were all working in silence. If a hand went up, the teacher came to help.

When she got back to Honus she asked him,

"Your ABC's, Honus, do you know the alphabet?"

Wide-eyed, he shook his head 'yes.' Anna Foster straightened up and clapped her hands, "Recess." The word got instant results. She put a hand on Honus's shoulder.

"Let's see you recite while the boys and girls are outside."

The alphabet was quickly done. The readers, one, two, and three as well.
Honus began to stumble on number four. Then there was arithmetic.

"Can you do your twos?" she asked. He did, then threes, fours and fives.
His memory served him well for arithmetic. The times tables came easy as
did simple division. What a mouthful, and it wasn't yet noon! She set Honus
to work on his Palmer Manual. There he had things to learn in penmanship.
The small muscles in a child's hand do not always do what they are told. The
Palmer Manual showed how to make letters and numbers. Honus struggled
to imitate. He was learning to write cursive, not print.

Later, when Mina met with Miss Foster, there was awe from Miss Foster
at Honus's skills. There was plenty to teach him, but he was out of step with
the others. Anna Foster, with a year of Normal School after high school, was
stumped. Her years of experience were with farm families where field work
came first and learning was incidental. Basic skills were all that was required.
Honus already had the basics; he needed more. She would need to find a way
to help this bright creature learn. What could she do?

At home, Honus had perched himself on his stool opposite the ironing
board.

"Mama, you went to school there, didn't you?" started it off.

Mina nodded affirmative. "I didn't go very long—there was work to do
at home."

"Were you little?" Honus asked.

Mina paused to switch irons. "I was six, like you," she said.

"Who was your teacher?" Honus wanted to know. "What was your
teacher like?"

Mina stopped to think. "It was so long ago."

"Was she nice?" asked Honus.

"No, Honus, it was a man. He was mean and I was afraid of him." A
flood of memories followed.

"He came in the fall, because, I guess nobody else wanted to teach. He was
tall and skinny, and he dressed like a preacher—all in black, with a string tie.
He talked different too. On the first day he told us his name was Emphalitius.
Us little girls giggled. But he rapped on his desk with a ruler and stared at us.
He told us we were not to call him by name, but to call him Master because
he was the School Master."

Honus saw fright and fear in his mother's face.

"He caught me," she said, "The first day of school he caught me writing
with my left hand. He whacked the ruler down on the desk real hard. He took
the pencil and put it in my right hand and he said, "Don't you ever write with

your left hand again! I never have, Honus. I don't have good handwriting, but he taught me right handed."

Honus looked at his mother. "Miss Foster is nice. She's not mean, but she sees everything."

Mina smiled; she knew about Anna Foster's special gift. She had one eye that had a muscle problem, so she really looked like she could see in two directions at once. Mina didn't give away her secret.

With Honus in school, it became easier for Mina to talk to him bout her own childhood. She had only attended school for three years. After that she was needed at home. Mina enjoyed her childhood memories. There were times when her gaze took her far away. Times when she saw herself as a child again. She told him of her sister Katie, barely a year younger, and their sheep herding in the stubble fields after harvest. For little girls to ride there were work horses, spavined old mares easy to bridle but hard to get on. The girls found a way. They put a handful of hay on the ground and when the horse lowered its head to eat, the little girls could shinny up its neck holding on to the horse's mane. Mina and Katie rode bareback, clinging to bridle and the horse's mane. Together the two little girls played through long days of work; milking morning and night, feeding chickens, cattle and sheep herding, carrying wood and water to the house.

"Everything but the pigs," their father told them, "Stay away from the pig pens."

Mina wistfully remembered her short-lived school days. How fearful she was of the master, Emphalitius. She remembered an older boy, Kitel Brunner, very slow to learn, with all the physical marks that made him easy to tease, big ears, drooping eyelids, a body that he had yet to grow into, stumbling and unsure of himself. Mina and Katie made fun of him at recess, pointed and hooted at his deformities. When he chased them, their quickness and agility only made him clumsier. Once he had told the teacher, who had only sneered at him and reminded him that they were little. That complaint had gotten him more attention than ever. The girls taunted,

Tattle tale, tattle tale
Hanging on the bull's tale
When the bull begins to pee
You can have a cup of tea.

In a rage Kitel had chased Mina into the girls' privy. He had followed her in and had threatened to stuff her through the toilet hole. Mina, scared witless, promised to leave him alone. The schoolmaster saw him leaving the girls' backhouse. He saw Mina's tearstained face and demanded that

Kitel explain. The boy could only stutter and stammer his embarrassment. The teacher hustled Kitel into the school house. No one dared enter until Emphalitius rang the bell to end recess. When they did go in, Kitel was at his desk. His big ears were a ruddy red. There were bruises on his face. He sat staring straight ahead the rest of the day.

At home his mother told him to go tend the trot lines on the riverbank. "Bring back enough fish for supper," she told him. Kitel never returned. His body, bloated and purple, still fully clothed, surfaced some miles downstream. He was buried beside an infant sister. His mother stood tearless, his father fidgeted as the grave was filled.

Mrs. Hogue, wrinkled and palsied, had sidled up to the Brunners. "Poor boy, he was a bother, wasn't he?" It was more than a question.

Old Brunner shook his head, "Ja, Ja," he said, "He won't bodder any more."

Mina saw her own actions exposed by Brunner's mean spirit. Honus sensed her anger. Telling Honus of the Brunner boy became a lesson even though a lifetime had intervened since a bratty little girl had teased a dull witted boy.

"Honus," she told him, "Be nice to kids at school." Then she added, "Don't ever go near the riverbank by yourself."

PART FOUR

Jensen

.22 STEVENS

The loft in the blacksmith shop was a conglomeration of worn-out abandoned, broken things that had accumulated from the time it was built. The old forge downstairs was still in use when there was a need, as was the grindstone. However, there were unused things like a double spring bear trap, a roll of binder wire and jars of stray nuts and bolts, along with worn-out horsecollars, harnesses, and worn hand tools that had been replaced. In the summer that he was six Honus discovered the loft. The only light came from a small gable window that was overgrown with cobwebs and dust. He found an old piece of burlap sacking to swish away the webs and wipe the windowpane. Though it was still gloomy, there was enough light to see what was in the loft. There were coffee cans that contained labels like 'skunk lard' and 'goose grease.' Next to the cans was a bottle labeled 'strychnine.' It was filled with white crystals and had a glass stopper which was waxed in place. Then, peering through the dimness, he saw it. Leaning against the wall in the far corner of the loft was a gun. It was so covered with grime that it was only a shape. He took it back to the light and took the burlap sack to it. Rubbing the gun stirred up so much dust that he retreated from the loft, down the ladder carrying the gun. It was clear that someone had greased the gun against rust and corrosion, and that would have been a very long time ago. When he had wiped it clean, Honus could see that there were missing parts. He didn't know the names of them until Lester told him later that there was no trigger guard, the front sight was missing, and there was no firing pin. Lester had laughed,

"Not much of a gun if you can't aim it or fire it."

Honus showed the gun to Mina, who did not like guns. She was on the verge of telling him he couldn't have it, when he told her what Lester had said.

"I guess it can't hurt anybody if it doesn't shoot, but you don't ever point it at anybody, hear?"

Lester gave the boy some kerosene to finish cleaning it. He put a nail on a string with bunting at the other end and showed the boy how to clean the barrel. Lester squinted down the barrel.

"That rifling looks like new," he said. "Too bad the rest of it can't be fixed."

For the boy it was enough. The gun had a trigger and a hammer. He could cock it and pull the trigger. All he got was a click, but he could stalk and pretend he was hunting.

One day as he wandered further along the riverbank than usual, gun under his arm as he had watched Lester carry his shotgun, he came to a clearing in a bend by the river. There was a small house with a porch that faced out toward the river. On the porch was a man sitting in a rocking chair. Beside him was a black and tan dog with a white belly. The man had seen the boy early on and was watching his progress. When he saw the boy looking his way, he waved. The dog started to get to his feet and gave a low growl.

"No, boy, down." The dog obeyed.

As the boy approached the man smiled, looking at the gun.

"Did you get anything?"

"Naw," replied the boy, "It's not a real gun. That is, it don't shoot. I just like to carry it."

The man leaned forward in his chair. His scalp was completely hairless; he had no eyebrows.

"Can I see your gun?" he asked.

Wordlessly, the boy handed him the gun. He laid it across his lap.

"This one's an old-timer, a Stevens twenty-two single shot. And you're right, it won't shoot without a firing pin."

The boy smiled, "That's what Lester said."

"Lester? Lester Sorby? Is he your brother?" "Well, sort of," the boy said.

"Oh, sorry, you must be Mina's boy, right?" The boy nodded affirmatively.

"Well, my name is Roald Jensen, and this here's Jubilo." He held out his hand to shake hands; the boy hesitated, then extended his hand for the first time in his life.

"People call me 'Old Man Jensen.' I don't much like it, but there it is. What's your name?" he asked.

"Honus, and I don't much like it either."

"You must be named after the baseball player, Honus Wagner, is that right?"

The boy nodded, "You know about him?"

Jensen nodded, "Well, sort of. He played for the Pittsburgh Pirates; he was a National League batting champion six or seven times."

The boy met those grey thoughtful eyes, "You know more about him than anybody has ever told me before."

Jensen smiled, "Who named you?"

"A man named Ted. He was my father."

Jensen let it go at that. "I know a little about guns. Maybe this one can be fixed up."

The boy couldn't believe what he was hearing. "Lester said it couldn't be fixed."

"Maybe so, maybe no. But if we can find a nail the same size as that breech, all we have to do is file it to fit and notch it in place."

After much rummaging in a toolbox, Jensen found a nail. Then he commenced a long and arduous filing and shaping process. When he finished, he slipped the pin in place, worked the ejector twice and handed the gun back to the boy.

"Now you need to understand that you can't go cocking and pulling the trigger the way you've been doing. This gun uses rim-fire ammunition. You'll ruin that firing pin unless you remember not to do that. Next time you come by we'll see if it works."

A look of pleasure, intense pleasure, crossed the boy's face.

"I don't like calling you 'Old Man Jensen.' Can I call you Mr. Jensen?"

Jensen grinned, "You don't like Honus; I'll call you Boy."

The small boy with a gun and the old young man shook hands again.

"You're sure I can come again, Mr. Jensen?"

"I'm sure you can, Boy."

When the boy came again, Jensen was guarded. "If this is a working gun, how do your folks feel about it?"

The boy had to say he didn't know. It wasn't a secret, he just hadn't talked about it.

Jensen paused, then said, "Well, let's do the drill. We'll see if it works, and if it does, we'll deal with it. Boy, twenty-two caliber shells come in short, long, and long rifle. Each speaks for itself. Short range, target practice; long range, small game if you're good. I've some shorts."

He took the boy out to his tool shed, mounted the gun in a vice. At five feet the gun was true. It pierced the target at exactly the same place each firing. As he lengthened the distance, the gun began to bear to the left. At thirty feet there was almost an inch of variance. The boy watched intently.

"Now what this means is you have to make allowances for that. But before you can allow for anything you need a sight out there on the end of that barrel."

The rear sight was there. It was adjustable with a screwdriver, but there was nothing else. Jensen puzzled over that. Finally, in his toolbox he found

a broken knife blade. He fixed it in place. Again, "Maybe so, maybe no."
He sighted along the barrel. Made some adjustments on the rear sight, and
tested it.

"About an inch to the left at thirty feet, no drop no rise. Try it."

With the gun secured firmly in the vise, the boy squinted through the
sights. He squeezed the trigger. For the first time he had fired a gun. His gun.
It fired true to Jensen's test shot. They tested it at forty feet, at fifty feet.

Then Jensen said, "Don't try to hit anything beyond fifty feet. You've
got the range."

In a few simple lessons, Jensen had taught Honus the allowances to make.
It was the simplest of weapons, but the rest of the variables were all human
judgment. A small boy, at six years old, held in his hand a deadly weapon.

When Honus told Lester what he had learned from Jensen, Lester was
surprised.

"Let's try it out."

The boy shook his head, "Can't, don't have any shells."

Lester did have some. They set a half-pint bottle on a fence post. Lester
went first. He missed the target but was surprised that the rifle even fired.
Honus had watched Lester; so when it came his turn, he paced off the distance
to the target, made his allowance and cut the bottle right down the middle.

Lester gasped, "Well I'll be damned."

When Mina found out about the gun, that it was a real weapon, she
worried. "He's just a little boy."

Lester didn't help much beyond assuring her that he would teach Honus
safety rules; how to climb through the strands of a barbed wire fence, what
to look for beyond a target, and the "never, nevers": you don't shoot song
birds, you don't ever squeeze the trigger without knowing why, and you never
ever point a gun at a person. Lester was a good teacher. He taught care and
he taught caution, to always respect your weapon, and to never take chances
with it.

"The thing that I don't like," Lester said, "is that the gun doesn't have a
trigger guard. That means you must be awful careful. Don't ever cock it unless
the stock is on your shoulder."

The day that Honus went off on his own with the gun, he never cocked
it, he never pointed it.

Honus went often to visit Mr. Jensen. Jensen was not a lonely man, but
he was a loner. Still, he and the boy became friends. Jensen was not well.
He had trouble breathing and a racking cough that sometimes left him
breathless. There were long silent times when Honus would simply sit with

Jensen. Jube now allowed himself to be petted and this was enough activity for all of them.

Jensen's other visitor was Ada Knutson Dirkson, Jensen's self-appointed guardian. He gave her money for groceries. His food appetites were scanty, easy to please. Sometimes, not often, he would drive to town with her. Ada was a gossip. When she came by, she talked a blue streak. She told him about the strange goings-on at Crazy Karl's place because she sort of looked out for him too. When she talked about Mina's boy, she said she felt sorry for him.

Jensen smiled at that, "Don't worry about him. He'll do fine."

Jensen liked Ada. She never talked about herself, but he knew she couldn't be having much of a life living with the Dirkson boys. Still, she weighed close to three hundred pounds so she couldn't be picky either. To himself, Jensen said, "Under all that fat is a heart of gold."

On good days when Jensen and the boy were together and talked, the boy asked questions. "How old is Jube?" "How come you named him Jube?" "Where are your kinfolk?"

"About Jube, I don't rightly know how old he is. He came here full-grown, but somebody had been real mean to him, and it took a while before we got things sorted out. About his name, there's a darkie song about the coming of the Lord. It's called 'In the Year of Jubilo.' So you see his name isn't really Jube, it's Jubilo." He smiled. "He doesn't mind if you call him Jube. I doubt he thinks much about such things. Neither do I."

"About my folks, when I went off to the war there was my daddy, my mama, and my sister Alice. They were all taken in the flu epidemic. All's left is me, and there's not too much of that." He must have known even then that he wouldn't get to be the "old man" that people already called him.

On one cool clear fall day when the boy came to visit, he found Jensen wearing his uniform tunic.

Jensen grinned, "Keeps me warm on mornings like this."

Honus didn't speak right away, but curiosity eventually prevailed.

"That's your army uniform, isn't it?" he asked.

Jensen nodded, "What I tell you about is all you'll need to know. This arm patch here is for the division I was in. We were called the Rainbows, that's what the patch shows."

Jensen looked off in the distance. For a while there was silence. When Jensen looked back at the boy his eyes were moist.

"These ribbons," he said, "some people call them 'fruit salad', some call 'em 'garbage.' Each one tells that you were in a battle; they're called campaign bars; others are called medals. If you were in a bad spot and you figured your way out of it, and if you were lucky, the army gave them as a sort of appreciation. See, this one is called the victory medal. Everybody in the army got one of those."

When the boy started to ask about the others, Jensen said, "That's all you need to know, boy."

Years later the boy would remember those bars with awe when he found them displayed in a book of military history. True to his word, Jensen told the boy all he needed to know. Jensen never mentioned them again.

JUBE AND ADA

When Jensen found him in his tool shed, he was a quivering mass of terror. He had a tin can tied to his tail and he had been bruised and rubbed with turpentine across his rear end. Jensen, being Jensen, had detached the can and bathed him and watched over him for days. The fear didn't go away for a long time. The bond between dog and man took a long time to grow. But once it did, these were two creatures whose strength was drawn from a source so strong that nothing could part them. From a fearful, cringing creature, Jube became a lion-hearted bundle of instinct only Jensen could direct.

When Stubby and Honus visited Jensen, he would be sitting on his chair on the porch. Jube would station himself between Jensen and his company. At first there had been a low gargling growl. Jensen would stop this with a touch and a word. As Jube became aware that they were not a threat to Jensen, he became more civil. Although he still watched from his sentry position, he would often even respond to a smile with an almost imperceptible wag of his tail. But he was not touchable; an extended hand, even in friendship, would get a wrinkling of his nostrils and a watchful eye. He was a natural retriever. Jensen kept a stick on the porch rail. "Fetch!" would bring up Jube's ears and tense his body into a coiled spring. Jensen, so limited in his own movement, kept Jube in good form by chasing the stick. It was inevitable that a small boy would want to play the game as well. When Honus threw the stick, Jube returned it to Jensen. This coaxed a laugh from everyone. The response caused Jube to jump up and down and furiously bark his approval. When Honus was finally able to intercept the stick, there was a violent boy-dog tug-of-war. Jube was exercised. Jensen was amused.

Ada Knutson Dirkson looked after Jensen as long as he lived. Ada was a Knutson girl whose two older sisters were bright, attractive girls while Ada was dull and unattractive. The Knutsons had sent the older girls to school in town where they had later worked, married well and moved away. Ada, the youngest, was a huge woman with small hands and small feet. She walked with a swaying motion as though she were wading waist deep in the river, but she had a basic, deep kindness about her. When Ole Knutson couldn't work his land any more, he hired the Dirkson boys. Inga Knutson had been "funny" for years before she died, so Ada held things together. When her father died the year after Inga, the older girls in an act of pity or generosity signed the farm over to Ada.

George and Paul Dirkson were two of a set of triplets. The third had died as a child. Stories were told that old Mrs. Dirkson had her triplets when she was in her late thirties. Too old to keep up with their demands and being a farmer's wife as well, she had pacified them with "sugar tits"; sugar tied in cheesecloth and dipped in whiskey. George and Paul were small, slightly built men. Hard workers when told what to do. Ada, a woman alone, needed them, so she and George went to town to the clerk's office and told him they wanted to get married. The clerk helped them fill out the license. Neither had done well in school to pass the county examination. Then he called the judge. Paul and a secretary were witnesses. George, Ada and Paul went home and did the evening chores. Ada had married George Dirkson without any fertility rites.

John and Gilbert had been weaned on whiskey. From babyhood they had an insatiable craving. It was to their advantage growing up during Prohibition. Since everyone was legally denied, everyone, man and boy alike, was illegally served. Ada understood. She knew how to home brew. Bottles lined her basement shelves. During the working season, spring planting, summer harvest, fall plowing, home brew was their mainstay. At the finish of planting and harvesting Ada went to her source and got them alky. She would cut the fiery proofage down. While she was doing her canning and preserving, she was also pickling her menfolk. They were there in the house where she could keep an eye on them. They stayed dead drunk until she sobered them up for their seasonal chores.

The Dirkson farm was a country mile from the river. The house, barn, sheds and pasture nestled in the corner at the intersection of two county roads. On high ground with good land, it was a productive quarter section. Ada asked questions, she watched what neighbors planted. She never asked for help, only advice. She was a familiar sight along the county road. She wore tent dresses, faded but usually clean, drove a "T" Ford, usually alone. Her great weight tilted the car to the driver's side.

When Roald Jensen came home from the war, Ada was among the first to visit. They had been children together in the old one-room school. She offered help, which Jensen graciously declined, a rejection which she graciously ignored. A loaf of fresh-baked bread, a pie, a jar of chokecherry jam would turn up on his porch with no explanation. Jensen understood kindness and accepted it. She offered to shop for his groceries, which he accepted. She noticed how careful he was with his money.

The Jensen farm was tucked into a bend of the river. The land had been fallow since Roald's parents had died. Would he want it spring toothed, Ada had asked. They soon had a share-crop arranged for his one hundred and twenty acres. Soon George and Paul were hard at work cultivating it. With almost twice the land to work, they looked ahead more than ever to the quenching of their thirst. The share arrangement was good for both of them.

Ada saw Jensen through the eyes of humble kindness. She remembered him as a bright, strong and free boy. Now in this short time he was old and ill, a bald shell of the boy she remembered. When she brought him his mail, she saw that he received a government check each month. On the rare occasions that she took him to town, he would ask her to take him to the bank.

When Ada saw Jube at Jensen's place, she recognized the dog. When Jensen told her about how he had found Jube, she thought it best to keep still. A dog so abused would never be much good. Still, Jensen's tenderness toward the dog brought tears to her eyes and she watched in amazement on successive visits at the change taking place in the dog. Finally she asked Jensen what he was going to call him.

Jensen, slow to smile, smiled, "Jubilo, I call him Jubilo."

Ada shook her head, "Funny name for a dog," she said.

"I heard it in an old darkie field song about the year of Jubilo."

"It's a funny name," Ada persisted.

"It's about the end of the world, Ada. That little critter faced it, so did I. When it comes we'll be there to meet it."

Jube lifted his head, cocked a quizzical ear and yawned. His instinct was to trust these two people, even if he didn't know what they were talking about.

As years passed Jensen placed more trust in Ada. He got out his uniform from the war, showed her his box of medals. They talked about his parents buried in the church yard. He said he could be buried in Arlington, but he didn't want that. While he explained that the National Cemetery was a special place, he said he wanted things plain: a pine box coffin, in his uniform, nothing else. Ada shushed him about dying.

"You'll outlive us all after what you've been through," she said.

But he didn't. Frosty winter weather, a chest cold that turned to pneumonia shut down his scarred lungs. Roald Jensen died in early spring. Ada had listened to his wracking cough days before. She wanted to get a doctor. Jensen would have none of it. He was feverish and subdued. Ada brought him chicken broth and tried to feed him. She sat with him through the night, dozing, waking, dozing. Jube's barking startled her awake. Jensen was propped on his elbows. He was giving orders to his men. Placing them to cover him. Then saying, "I'm going after him." He fell back on the bed with a great guttural groan. He was dead.

Jube's bark became a whine. He lay down at the foot of the bed, head between his paws, knowing but not wanting to know.

Ada sobbed, sighed, and covered Jensen's body with a sheet. She looked at Jube.

"You stand guard, Jube," she said, knowing full well that Jube was going nowhere.

Ada brought back George and Paul. Together they lifted Jensen to the kitchen table. Ada washed his stiffening body and dressed him in his uniform. Then George and Paul put him back on the bed. Jube had allowed all this. Jensen's stillness warned him not to interfere. The Dirksons left; when they returned, they trailed a pine coffin behind the tractor. Tenderly they lifted Jensen's stiffened body into the coffin. Jube watched every move.

By the next day news of Jensen's death had made the rounds. The Tedeman boys would dig the grave. A day hence the minister could be there to make it a Christian burial.

Jube watched a succession of people come and go, paying their respects to a man most of them barely knew. There was awe when they looked at the young man with the old face. He was the mysterious loner who had now found peace. Mina, Lester, and Honus had gone. Ada had winked at the boy and tried to smile. She knew the bond between the boy and the man. Honus wept and ground his tears into his eyes. Jensen wouldn't like tears. Jube had kept his place by the coffin. Ada warned people that he wasn't friendly. The few who tested her warning were rewarded with a low growl. When Honus held out his hand, he got a tail wag from Jube and a "well I never," from Ada.

The minister at graveside gave the few remarks that the sacrament called for. On a cold March afternoon, Roald Jensen was laid to rest beside his father and mother.

People gathered afterwards at the old Dirkson farm, now called "Ada's Place." There was prepared food as always after a funeral. To no one's surprise Ada had gone to her source and had drinks. George and Paul stood by the door and dispensed it from clear glass jugs into tin drinking cups. "Powerful stuff," was said more than once. When the day ended and families drifted away, Ada cleaned up the kitchen. She worked alone. George and Paul were dead to the world in the parlor. Finished and weary from the long day, she sat down to rest. Then startled, she exclaimed, "What happened to Jube?"

What happened to Jube was that he had guarded the coffin and had followed it when it was taken away. He had watched the funeral, watched the lowering of the coffin, and the filling of the grave. When people left, he resumed his guard. Ada had searched Jensen's house and had called to no avail. By chance she went to the graveyard and saw Jube there. No amount of coaxing would move him. From that day on, it became part of her daily ritual to bring him something to eat, a bowl of milk, table scraps, whatever was handy. She never saw him eat or drink, and there was always something left when she brought more. Jube watched her and occasionally wagged his appreciation, but never left his post. He grew thinner and shabbier as the months passed. Anna Foster watched from the schoolhouse across the road.

"A grieving dog will die," she said."

"I made a promise to look after him," was all that Ada said she could do.

When Ada went to Jensen's mailbox and found his government check was there, she didn't know what to do with it. She knew about his trips to the bank, so she took it to town to the bank. When she told the teller her reason for coming, he quickly summoned the banker. The banker was a fat florid Dutchman named Lundeen, "Mr. Lundeen" to everyone. No one even knew his first name. Ada told him of Jensen's death. When he asked for details, she told him about Jensen's dying wishes, and what she had done. When the teller brought him Jensen's account sheet he was more than perplexed.

"Roald Jensen named Ada Knutson Dirkson, that's you, as his beneficiary."

Ada was a blank. "What does that mean?" she wanted to know.

"It means he wants you to have his money," said Lundeen. "But it's not all that simple. There was no doctor in attendance, no death certificate. He has a deposit here in the bank that can only be opened with his key and one from the bank."

Ada thought about that. "Jensen had a box of medals from the war that he wanted buried with him," said Ada. Lundeen groaned.

"But," Ada continued, "He left one medal out for a little boy, Mina's boy," she said, "and a key. He said that key is for you when the time comes."

Lundeen sized her up, "She's as honest and kind as the day is long," he thought. A banker's judgment earns his reputation.

"This may take a while," he said. "The first thing is to notify the government about the check. We can help you with that if you say so."

"Oh, please do," pleaded Ada. "I don't know anything about government things."

Lundeen stood, extended his hand and said, "We'll see what happens."

What happened was about a week later, a man in uniform came to the farm. He came asking about Jensen, where he lived, the cause of his death, where he was buried. Ada answered these questions and took him to the graveyard. He looked at the grave and at Jube and shook his head.

"That man could have been buried in Arlington Cemetery in Washington, D.C. with full military honors, attended by top brass and high mucky mucks." Ada nodded, "Yes, he said that before he died, but he didn't want anything fancy. That's the way he was."

The officer explained that since there was no death certificate there needed to be an affidavit verifying Jensen's death. They drove to town to the county clerk's office where the clerk very reluctantly helped them. The Army officer kept the original and insisted on a copy with the county seal for Ada. Flustered, she accepted his help and thanked him several times. He drove her back to the farm, tipped his hat and drove away.

Ada waved and then caught her breath. "I never even asked him his name. Ada, you're not very smart," she said to herself.

When Ada went to town and showed the affidavit to Lundeen, the banker eyed her with a new respect.

"You've saved yourself a whole lot of fol-de-rol with this affidavit," he said. When she explained how it had all happened, he was curious and asked a number of questions before he got to the bank's business.

"You have a legal right to look in the deposit box. This letter makes that possible. I can accompany you as you really should have a witness."

Ada happily agreed. Lundeen inserted the bank key and pointed for Ada to insert hers. When she pulled out the drawer there were only papers. Jensen's army discharge was wrapped around the letters that went with his medals. Beneath was an envelope with her name on it. She opened it and stared blankly. She handed it to Lundeen.

"It looks like a government insurance policy," he said. "Most service men dropped their insurance when they came home and the war was over, apparently Jensen didn't." Lundeen thumbed through the policy. "Ada, you are the beneficiary. That means you get the money from it."

"My stars," Ada had tears in her eyes. "Jensen, you didn't have to do that!"

Lundeen smiled, "He sure enough wanted you to have it." "Is it much?" she asked. Lundeen pointed to the figure on the policy.

"How much is that?" asked Ada.

Lundeen eyed her quizzically, "Ten thousand dollars," he said.

Ada gasped, "My God, all I ever wanted to do was help him. My men and me, we all pitched in and worked his land, but he shared for that."

Lundeen was thoughtful. "The farm, yes, there will be a title to that somewhere in the courthouse. If you want I can search it for you." "Oh, yes, I would be so obliged. We would rent from whoever owns it."

As Ada was leaving the bank, Lundeen asked her about Jensen's account. "You are named the beneficiary on that too."

Ada was at an emotional overload. "Oh, Mr. Lundeen, I'd just like to keep it here with you. Is that all right?"

Lundeen smiled, "We always welcome a new customer."

DECORATION DAY

The Beavertail River curled around the North Beavertail Lutheran Church. The graveyard was fenced on both sides and in back of the church. Log rails in front of the church left a parking area from the church to the high road. This spring there was a fresh grave. Roald Jensen, a local boy, had been the first veteran of the Great War to die. It was his wish to be buried here with his people rather than in a national cemetery. The Tedeman boys, Marcus, Marvin, and Benny, had dug his grave. It meant cutting through the frosted loam and down to the clay which lay beneath. They were all strapping big men. They dug with spades and grubbing mattocks. The roots of an old elm were cleared away as they descended. At eye level they had reached six feet. On a ladder they climbed out, heavy with sweat.

The Reverend Gunder Fagin officiated at the graveside. Private Jensen was in uniform. The coffin was plain pine. He had a rainbow patch on his sleeve and one small bar on his chest. Under his right arm was an old White Owl cigar box. Ada Dirkson had tended his body, washed and dressed him for his funeral. She had done what he had asked before he died.

The Reverend Fagin had praised him as a fallen hero, a patriot, a man who had fought for the glory of his country. He had spoken in general terms as he barely knew who Jensen was. Roald Jensen was not a man who spent time with a preacher.

Now comes Decoration Day. There was to be a program planned by Anna Foster, the schoolteacher, and the Reverend Gunder Fagin. People would come out of respect for Jensen. There would be a recitation by one of Miss Foster's pupils, and the preacher would give an inspirational requiem for his friend the fallen hero. School ends after Decoration Day. Boys are needed in the fields; girls in the kitchen. Anna tried out the recitations with the children still in school, mostly little ones. She came up with only one who could memorize and recite. When she talked to the minister, he was less than pleased.

"That child should not be your example. Really, how could you want him to show off in front of our congregation?"

Anna looked away, "The boy knew Roald Jensen. They were dear to each other, and he's the only one who can memorize and recite a poem."

The preacher shook his head, pursed his lips, "Maybe we don't need any schoolchildren."

Anna sighed, "It's not his fault he is what he is. If this is the only life he has, why can't we help him live it?"

The preacher shook his head, "People will talk. They'll say we chose an illegitimate child over their own baptized ones."

Anna shrugged, "Children are children. He's the smartest little boy I ever taught."

"Let me think on it," said the preacher.

The week went by. On Thursday before school ended the minister stopped by the schoolhouse.

"I haven't come up with anything," he said, "I suppose it's too late for the boy to recite on Saturday."

Anna smiled, "I don't think so. Tell me if you want him to recite."

The preacher looked startled, "What would he recite?"

"It's a poem about the war, maybe you've heard it, it's called 'In Flanders Fields.'"

"Can't say I have, Flanders is in Europe, isn't it?"

"Yes," said Anna, "It's where Roald Jensen fought his war."

The preacher nodded, "If you think he can do it, let's go ahead."

"Do you want to hear him?" Anna asked.

"No, I'll take your word for it." He turned to leave. "Saturday morning, ten o'clock, maybe only a few will come."

Quite a few came; Roald Jensen was Danish. That was Scandinavian enough to draw a Lutheran crowd. Men dressed to work in the fields; women eyeing each other for new dresses. Children crowded to the front to see the program. Their teacher, Miss Foster, was there with them, still in charge. Ada Knutson Dirkson stood nearby, too. She had visited Jensen's grave almost daily since his burial; not because of Roald, but to care for his old dog Jube who had taken up a guardian space next to the grave. Although Ada kept him fed and watered he was pretty much skin and bones from his long vigil.

As people gathered for the service, a car with a government license and two uniformed men rattled across the wood plank bridge. They pulled off to one side, carefully avoiding the crowd. There were curious stares, but no overtures. Finally, however, the minister had bustled over and introduced himself.

The sergeant explained, "Sergeant Reeves and Private Davis, we're here to put a flag on the grave of Private Roald Jensen. Orders from our commanding officer, Major Anderson."

The minister was impressed. "Well, his neighbors have come to pay their respects and honor him too. We are proud that you have come."

The program was shaping up better than he had expected. "We have a memorial planned, please join us." The preacher raised his voice. "These fine men are in the service of our country. They too have come to pay homage to our fallen hero. They've driven all the way from Minneapolis, from the fort, what was it?"

The sergeant cleared his throat, "Snelling, Fort Snelling. We brought a flag to post over his grave."

People nodded their approval and then, since everyone was standing, shifted from one foot to the other.

The preacher began, "We also have a poem to be recited by one of Miss Foster's pupils." He then launched into a eulogy of Roald Jensen, "Our dear friend, beloved by all." It was fairly brief since he had barely ever met the man. "And now Miss Foster, will you introduce your program."

While the teacher explained that the poem to be recited was about a military cemetery in Europe, Ada Knutson Dirkson had gone up to the small boy standing by his teacher. She hung a ribbon and a medal around his neck. It hung almost to his waist.

"And now," the teacher said, "The poem is called in 'In Flanders Fields.'"

The small piping voice began, "In Flanders Fields, by James McLean."

> In Flanders fields where poppies blow
> Between the crosses row on row
> That mark our place
> And in the sky
> The larks still bravely singing fly . . .

The silence of the crowd magnified the song of a meadowlark in the distance. The rustling of the elm that shaded them, the very sounds that were no sounds, the grass, the river, the sun itself.

The army sergeant squinted and edged closer. "Do you see what that kid is wearing?"

The private looked, "Yeah, bib overalls and a shirt."

Exasperated, the sergeant said, "No, the ribbon around his neck, and the medal."

The private shrugged, "What about it?"

The sergeant looked at him, "That ribbon and that medal he's wearing is the Congressional Medal of Honor."

"How do you suppose he got that?" asked the private.

The sergeant shook his head, "I don't know, but I'm sure it's got something to do with why we're here."

The boy had touched the crowd, that was clear. When he finished,

> If you break faith with us who died
> We shall not sleep though poppies blow
> In Flanders fields.

There were women wiping their eyes, and men looking down at the ground. There was no applause. This was religious or the minister wouldn't be there. Ada whispered something in his ear. Miss Foster patted him on the shoulder and said, "Well done."

The two soldiers edged forward. "That was very good, son. Can I ask you something? Where did you get that medal?"

Ada answered for him, "Roald wanted him to have it. He had a whole box of medals."

"Where are they?" asked the sergeant.

Ada pointed to the grave, "They're buried with him. That's what he wanted. There was a letter, too, signed by the president—you know, the president of the United States."

The sergeant asked, "Do you have the letter?"

Ada had the letter. "It's for the boy too." She handed it to him. The sergeant gave it his undivided attention for several minutes.

Meanwhile the preacher returned from his people. Looking at the medal, he said, "Perhaps this is something we should all share."

The sergeant said, "If Private Jensen wanted the boy to have it, I would reckon it should be his." The minister left it there.

"The letter," the sergeant spoke to Ada, "It's about my commanding officer, could I take it and show it to him?" Wordlessly, Ada handed it to him.

Farmers were heading back to the fields. A flag as a headstone stood above Roald Jensen's grave.

"I liked your poem, son. I'm sure Private Jensen would have liked it too." The boy's eyes brimmed with tears, "He was my friend, him and me and old Jube, we were best friends."

The sergeant was touched by the boy's emotion. He squatted down to eye level with the boy. "Who's Jube?"

Wordless, the boy pointed to the dog lying next to Jensen's grave.

"Funny name for a dog," the private said.

The boy spoke up, "His real name is Jubilo, Old Man Jensen said that. The year the kingdom was a-comin' was the year of Jubilo. It was a song he used to play on his mouth organ."

"That's quite an honor he left you . . . But he really wasn't very old."

The boy's face lit up, "People just called him 'old man' because he didn't have any hair, not one hair on his head. He said it happened during the war, but he never talked about it."

By now it was noon. Farmers and their families were home for dinner. The minister was giving his attention to Ada and Anna. The sergeant went over to where Jube was lying, but when he extended his hand to pet him, he got a low growl.

"Still standing guard, aren't you, old fella."

The boy came over and scratched Jube's ear. Jube tilted his head toward the scratch.

"My mama said he could come home and be my dog, but he won't leave." The sergeant scratched his chin. "He's far too weak to go any distance, but if you could put a lead on him maybe we could get him to the car and take him to your place."

"What's a lead?" the boy asked.

"A rope, or a strap, or something, I think I got some in the car. Private, have we got a short piece of rope?"

Private Davis returned with a cord. The sergeant made a slipknot and handed it to the boy.

"Put it around his neck, but not too tight."

Jube lifted his head and the boy slipped the cord around his neck.

"So far, so good," The sergeant grinned. "Now will he come with you?"

Jube got up weak and wobbly and walked to the car. He even let the sergeant help him into the back seat.

"How about that! Somehow he knows his job here is done." The sergeant turned to the boy, "Climb in there beside your dog, son, and tell us where you live."

The preacher came over and thanked the army men effusively. "You men added a great deal to our program, and we do thank you for coming." He looked into the back seat, grimaced and said, "And thank you too for getting rid of that dog."

The sergeant stiffened a little. He and the private climbed into the front seat.

"Now tell us where you live, son."

"I can show you," he pointed across the bridge they had crossed earlier. When they came to the section road, he pointed left.

"When you come to our mailbox you can see our house down the road. At the mailbox they turned. Sorby was the name on the mailbox.

"You a Sorby?" asked Private Davis.

"My mama is," responded the boy.

It was a big square white two story house. A woman wearing an apron stepped out onto the porch, closing the screen door behind her.

"That's my mama," said the boy.

Seeing the boy, she hurried toward the car.

"Missus Sorby?" asked the sergeant.

"Yes?" she said.

Seeing her worried look he hastened to explain. "We were over at the church for the Decoration Day service. Your boy spoke a piece, and we got kind of interested. You see, we were sent here from Fort Snelling in Minneapolis to put a flag on Private Jensen's grave."

"Honus, where did yo get that thing around your neck?"

"Ada gave it to me. Mr. Jensen wanted me to have it."

"What is it?"

The sergeant answered, "It's a medal, ma'am, a very important medal. It's the highest honor a soldier can get. He must have thought a lot of your boy."

"Hoan, you be careful with it," she said.

The boy pointed, "I got Jubilo too, mama."

"I spose you want to keep him," she shook her head. "Well, you'll have to take care of him, he looks pretty sickly to me."

The sergeant smiled, "Poor old thing's been sitting by that grave for three months or more. I don't think anybody but your boy could have coaxed him away."

"He's always coming home with something." She turned to the boy, "Take him up on the porch, we'll see if he'll eat."

As the boy walked away the sergeant watched, "Your boy, you call him Honus?"

"Yes," she said, "It's a funny name. His father named him; said he was named after some baseball player. I call him 'Honee' most of the time."

"Well, ma'am, we've got a ways to go, so we better get started." They climbed back into the car. Mina thanked them for bringing the boy home.

They waved, "Goodbye, son, take good care of Jensen's medal. And take good care of old Jube, too."

As Mina came back to the house, Jube managed a feeble wag of his tail. Mina sighed, "Sitting there by that grave all this time; I thought for sure you were a goner. Honee, if he doesn't make it, you'll be to blame."

The boy grinned, "He'll make it."

Mina Sorby was a good cook. No one ever left her table unsatisfied. Thus Jube was dining on trimmings and first cuts. The boy hand fed him, and he prospered mightily. By midsummer he was steady, almost frisky. Also he had put his grief for Jensen behind him. His loyalty now was to the boy: Jube had a bed under the porch at night, but his days were spent in sunlight. By the wooded river they hunted and fished. They wrestled and had sham battles until they were exhausted, then would lie in the shade to recoup. Roald Jensen indeed lived on with his best of friends.

MAJOR ANDERSON

Highway Six was two miles by section roads from the farm. From there the two soldiers took the main highway for the lengthy trip, arriving at Fort Snelling in deepening twilight. The duty clerk had left them a note to report to the CO at 0800.

Scrubbed, shaved but still sleepy, they stood at attention before his desk. Major Anderson was spit-and-polish military, so the men were surprised when he said, "At ease men, take seats." Once they were seated, he asked,

"How did it go?"

Sergeant Reeves told him about the program and about the boy in some detail. When he got to the letter and the medal, the major leaned forward, attentive. When the sergeant produced the letter and handed it to Major Anderson, the major shifted back in his chair to read it. The non-com sensed that this was an emotional thing with the major. The room had a special silence, a poised kind of hush. The major started to speak, paused, took a breath, tried again.

"Roald Jensen was barely nineteen when he came to the Rainbows. I barely had my bar when he was assigned to my platoon." The major was speaking slowly, almost talking to himself, lost in another time.

"He was this grass-green kid from northern Minnesota. I was this puffed-up shavetail fresh from West Point. But that's another story. Jensen was so quiet, shy maybe, that he took a ribbing over just about everything he did. He was a good kid, took it all in, laughed it off. He was smart; took instruction well, and when we got out on the firing range, there was nobody like him. I remember asking him once how he learned to shoot.

"Sir," he said, "I've had a gun ever since I was a little kid. Hunted all my life."

"When the Rainbows shipped out in April of '17, we were in the thick of it until the war ended. Jensen had this old Enfield that he cared for like a baby. He gained everybody's respect because he never ran out of ammunition. He was that selective of his target. He could spot a movement the size of a penny and drill it from a hundred yards. The trenches were rotten, miserable—you've heard all that. Jensen was not a leader, but he was an inspiration. He never went after a medal, but he ended up the most decorated man in the battalion. This letter," the major pointed to the letter on the desk, "I helped write it. I never knew it would get this far. Field headquarters carried it on, I guess. One thing's for sure. I wouldn't be here but for him." The major gazed thoughtfully over their heads before he continued.

"I had an order to reconnoiter an area between two hilly slopes to determine if advancement was possible from where we were dug in. It was a blind pocket. No way to know or even guess about Kraut positions along those slopes. We knew the war was almost over, but for some Germans that only made them more stubborn. I could have asked any man in the platoon, but I didn't. After a year in the trenches, I guess you look for excitement. Anyway, I went for it myself. Stripped down to skivvies, a .38 and a handful of rounds and climbed out into the tall grass. The wind was blowing toward me to my advantage for concealment, or so I thought. The platoon was dug in to cover me. About two hundred yards out the grass became sparse and shorter. Time to go back. Then they cut loose. Krauts were positioned on both slopes. They had me in a crossfire, pinned down with nowhere to go. I had taken a shot in the hip; I think they figured me for dead. I did too. From there on I can only guess how he did it, but Jensen got behind one of the positions and one by one picked off every Kraut in the nest. Then he apparently loaded their machine gun and aimed at the other position. They came out with their hands up, except for one. He lobbed a canister and then another one. One was phosgene, the other was mustard gas. Phosgene is colorless, but you can see mustard gas creep along the ground with the wind. Jensen opened up on them. The only one alive was the one who had thrown the canisters. He was dug in waiting for the gas to do its work. Whatever Jensen did with his first shot caused the Kraut's machine gun to explode. As the Kraut jumped away from the explosion, Jensen's second shot killed him. Jensen could see the poison gas moving toward me. He had to go through it to get to me. He had put on his gas mask and ran to beat the cloud. It was almost a tie. When he got to me, he stripped off the gas mask and put it on me and dragged me back to the trench. Then he cleared the platoon out of the path of the gas and came back and got me. Men from the platoon told me that his hands and face were blistered from the mustard gas. Worst of all, when he took off his helmet every hair on his head came out. I'm sure that's why he got the nickname, 'Old Man Jensen.' His war days were over. His lungs burned and scarred. When they sent us home, he was still in the hospital. I saw him there when we were released. I remember him saying, 'I'm glad you made it, sir.' As of now, I guess I made it. He didn't."

"Men, I appreciate your carrying my respects to Jensen. He was one helluva soldier."

"I'll keep the letter."

PART FIVE

Compassion and Revenge

MITZI

Somewhere on the very edge of the boy's memory there was Mitzi. She was the family mouser. White with angora fur, Mitzi was not domesticated. She patrolled the barn, moving like a white shadow through the machine shed and the blacksmith shop. Even Mina could not remember a time when Mitzi had not been around.

Somewhere in the darkness in early spring Mitzi either succumbed or was forced into a romantic interlude with a truly wild creature, one rarely seen and owing allegiance to no one. When her kittens were born, she carefully concealed them in the loft of the blacksmith shop. There she made nest of old toweling, binder twine and lint.

Mitzi trusted the boy and accepted him when he found her secret place. Mitzi mothered her five little kits. The boy visited them every day. He brought her food, especially milk. Her little ones were insatiable. After a week their eyes were beginning to open. None of them favored their mother. They were all tiger striped, tiny and soft. Honus thought about giving them names.

On the ninth day when Honus climbed to the loft, he found a shambles. Disemboweled kittens, a leg, a head, bloodied guts, and the evidences of a battle, tufts of Mitzi's angora hair, and chunks of a tiger cat's fur.

Honus found Mitzi cowering in a dark corner. She was not badly injured, but defeated with an unmistakable animal dejection. Honus picked her up and carried her to the house. Crying himself he told Mina what had happened.

"Tom cats do that, Honus, don't ask me why. They just do."

Honus coaxed poor Mitzi to eat to no avail. She wandered aimlessly toward the barn and then toward the blacksmith shop. Honus saw where she as headed and went up to the loft and cleaned up the horrid mess before she got there.

A day went by before the agony began. Honus heard her cries and followed the sound. When he found her she was stretched full length in the bed she had made for her kittens. Tenderly, the boy picked her up and carried her to the house. Mina saw the problem. Her little teats were as hard as a board.

"She's milk-bound. If it doesn't go away she'll die." Mina had tears in her eyes. "If only one of her kittens had lived, she'd be all right."

Mina wondered later in the day where the boy was. He hadn't said a word. What he had done was scour the neighborhood, first the Hogues, then the Tilsens, then the Tedemans, finally as the day was wearing on, at Fritz Lohmann's. Each place he had asked if there was a kitten he could have. Until he got to Fritz's there were none. Fritz's wife was Hulda, stern and not friendly. She listened to his story, put on her overcoat and took his hand. They walked to the barn. There in a manger was a cat curled up with her five kittens. Hulda lifted out a tiny black kitten and handed it to Honus. He gasped out his thank you and ran the half mile home. Mitzi was in a box by the kitchen door when he laid the kitten next to her. Hungry, it nuzzled its way into her bulging teats. There was soon contentment. Mina saw the boy squatting by Mitzi's box. "Where in heaven's name have you been?" she asked.

Honus didn't answer. He pointed.

"Where did you get the kitten?"

Honus stood up. He looked at his mother. "I'm going to name it Hulda." Then she knew.

HULDA

Mitzi had her box and her kitten in the basement next to the warmth of the furnace. Having the full source of nourishment all to itself, the kitten prospered mightily. Also it bonded closely with Mitzi. Tongue washes were such a ritual that the kitten was shiny and spotless.

Lester was the first to notice as the kitten grew.

"Boy, you're going to have to give your kitten another name."

Honus was mystified; "What you talkin' about?"

Lester grinned, "Well, your Hulda-cat's got balls. She's a he." Lester thought it was funny. Honus did not.

"It's gonna be a he-Hulda instead of a she-Hulda, that's all."

As Hulda grew, it became clear that this was no ordinary animal. Hulda outgrew Mitzi in a matter of months. Full grown, Hulda was two of Mitzi, but Mitzi was dominant. This was a mother-son relationship that was strong. Still, Honus was a part of it. He remembered Mitzi's agony when she lost her brood, and he knew that the gray tiger-cat was somewhere in the neighborhood, honed with instincts that sensed the natural order of life.

Mitzi shunned the loft in the blacksmith shop. She and Hulda became barn cats. There was no scarcity of mice, sparrows, even pigeons. Hulda's prowess as a hunter was easy to see. If Mitzi failed to provide for herself, Hulda saw to it. Hulda even brought Honus an occasional mouse, much to Mina's disapproval.

Eventually there was the inevitable return of the tiger-tom, answering his primeval urge. He was a powerful tawny creature who must have sensed the presence of Hulda. He had come for Mitzi, and it was her he stalked. Hulda was young and untested, but the sounds and smells of a thousand generations of fighters came into play when the low rattling growl and the twitching tail took shape in the darkness. The tiger sprang with slashing claws and fangs. Hulda stood his ground. The searing pain brought the reality. This was life or death. The old veteran came screaming and clawing again, but soon was aware that he was outweighed and outreached by a younger cat that moved like liquid lightning. When he turned to escape, Hulda rode him to the ground where he turned on his back to fight off his attacker, but to no avail. Hulda tore open his belly and slashed his neck. He crawled to the edge of the riverbank and there he died.

When Honus came to the barn next morning he found Mitzi carefully washing Hulda's wounds. Lester came as well.

"Must have been one helluva fight."

He looked around and saw the trail of blood from the old tiger cat. Lester and Honus followed the blood to the riverbank where they found him. Lester edged his boot under the cat's body and pushed him into the stream.

"Good riddance," he said.

Honus watched the floating body.

"He had it coming," he said.

OLD GREY

Lester had a no-nonsense approach to farm animals. When an old ewe abandoned her lamb, he would try to pair it up with another ewe; and if that didn't work, he killed the lamb. That spring a ewe gave birth very early. When she refused her lamb, Lester was really exasperated. He talked with Mina about it while the boy listened. When Lester said he'd have to kill the lamb and be done with it, the boy piped up.

"No, let me feed him. I'll do it from a bottle."

Lester shook his head. "That sounds good fun for a few days, but then you'll be tired of it. Then I'll have to kill it anyway."

Mina hung her head. "You want me to tell you what to do, don't you. Well, Honee, if you take it on, there will be no backing off."

Lester looked on in disgust.

"I'll make him a rubber tit. Honee can feed him in the morning and when he gets home from school. Lester, you make him a pen by the kitchen porch. Jubilo can keep an eye on him. He won't hurt him."

With the double challenge from his mother and from Lester, the boy took care to feed the lamb warm milk and watch over it. Jube got the idea that the lamb needed a guard. He even chased curious chickens away. The lamb was doing fine, wagging his tail and bleating when he saw the boy coming with his milk bottle. He was always ravenous, nudging the bottle in the way a lamb would go after its mother's milk.

In several weeks it was clear that the lamb was not only surviving but prospering. Lester was saying it was about time to get it back to the flock.

"It's starting to stink up the place."

Honus knew he was right. "When? Tomorrow? I'm still going to watch out for him. I did save him, you know," he grinned at Lester.

Lester glared, sort of, but said nothing. In the early dawn the next morning, they were all awakened by Jube's furious barking and the bleating scream of the lamb. Lester was first with his shotgun. He thundered away at the grey shadow as it disappeared over the riverbank.

"Damn old grey," he said.

The lamb was dead. Jube was bleeding from a slash in his shoulder. The wild dog that had become a legend as a sheep killer was long gone when the boy got up from the steps. Mina had gotten pine tar salve and doctored Jube's wound. Jube was a mix of hound and terrier and Old Grey was at least five times his size, but in a fight Jube was twenty pounds of pure instinct and fury. He would have fought to the last drop of blood. Lester cleaned up the dead lamb and buried it. He took down the pen.

Mina was wiping her hands on her apron when Lester came in.

"It don't pay to make pets out of farm animals, you just end up getting hurt because one way or another they always die."

He sat down by Honus at the table. Honus, his head bowed, was silent.

Lester said, "It wasn't your fault. That old wild dog has been doing that for years. He's like a ghost. Even with a shotgun I never touched him."

Mina looked at the two of them, "You boys aren't much alike. That lamb wasn't a farm animal to Honus, Lester. It was a friend. Now how about breakfast?" Lester agreed.

The boy looked at them, one to the other. "Old Grey is going to die for this."

Lester looked quizzical. Mina started to speak, then thought better of it. They ate breakfast in silence except for Lester scrunching his cornflakes with his big hands before he poured milk over them.

There was still snow on the ground and freezing nights Honus followed the tracks to where Lester had buried the lamb in a snowbank. The lamb had literally been torn to pieces by the savage dog. The shape of a hind leg was visible in the snow. The boy dug it out. The flesh was cold as he skinned it with his pocketknife. Honus made slits in the flesh of the lamb and embedded old single-edge razor blades. The razor blades, used for scraping, were kept in the blacksmith shop.

"Just like the Eskimos," he said to himself. He followed Old Grey's footprints in the snow to a river bend that had a scrap iron pile. Rusting farm equipment had accumulated there for years. It was a favorite place to hunt rabbits in the winter, ground squirrels, chipmunks and woodchucks in the summer. The old dog's tracks had gone beyond the scrap heap, but with rabbits around he might come back. The lamb's leg was stiffening in the freezing snow. Maybe Old Grey was watching from some concealment. Maybe his hunger overcame his fear of the scent of a small boy. Somewhere in the night that followed, the wild dog came back to the scent of the dead lamb. By then the meat would be stiff but not frozen. He would pick it up in his jaws, lick it, and taste blood, lick more. Finally, weak, he would seek cover.

The following morning Honus told his mother he was going after rabbits. His .22 single-shot was a relic, but it usually worked. This morning he slid down the high riverbank and followed the river to the bend and the scrap pile. He saw that the lamb leg had been moved, pulled, carried some distance through the snow. Then he saw the blood, droplets in the snow, then bigger drops. Following the river bend by bend, he came to the Hugness bridge. There he saw Old Grey under the bridge.

As he approached, the dog tried to raise his head. His tongue, a mass of ragged slivers, lolled from his mouth. His grey eyes were still alive with a wild hatred, but they were also glassy and unfocused. The boy cocked his rifle and brought it within inches of the dog's head. He pulled the trigger. The gun misfired. He cocked again and pressed the trigger. This time it fired, leaving a small hole between Old Grey's eyes.

"Now we're even. You killed the lamb, the lamb killed you."

As Honus followed the road back to the farmyard, he saw Lester working in the machine shed. He was overhauling the old Allis Chambers tractor. Parts were laid out on sheets all around the tractor. When the boy came through the door, Lester yelled.

"Look where you're going. Don't step on any of that stuff."

The boy carefully picked his way to where Lester was working. Lester was wearing old OshKosh coveralls; his hands were greasy. Noticing the gun he asked, "Did you get anything?"

Honus nodded, "I just shot Old Grey."

Lester laughed, "Sure and I'm a monkey's uncle."

"Really, Lester, I did. You want to see him?"

Lester, realizing the boy meant what he said, asked, "Where is he?"

"Down by the Hugness bridge."

Lester said, "Show me."

Lester, in his greasy overalls, and Honus, carrying his rifle, headed for the bridge. Lester looked at the dead dog.

"Big, must be close to a hundred pounds. How'd you get near enough to shoot him?"

When Honus explained how he had used the lamb's leg and the razor blades, Lester looked closer at Old Grey's tongue. He saw that it was slivered all to pieces.

"Jesus, how'd you ever think of a thing like that?"

The boy said, "It's in my Circle book. That's the way the Eskimos kill wolves. Only the wolves kill each other when they smell blood."

Lester poked the body with his foot. "What a godawful way to die," he said.

Honus looked at him. "No worse than what he did to the lamb."

When Lester talked with his mother, he told her very quietly what had happened. She listened, took it all in. Lester continued.

"It all comes out of that book. He shouldn't have anything that gives him ideas like that. He shouldn't have a gun either. He's not old enough."

They sat at the kitchen table. Mina leaned on the table, her head in her hands, her eyes closed.

"He has the book and he has the gun, and he used them both to kill Old Grey. Everybody around here has tried to kill that dog; traps, poison, even a posse once when he killed so many of the Krabbenhoff's sheep, remember?" She looked at Lester, "He outsmarted Old Grey, son. If that dog wouldn't have come around, he would never even have thought of it."

Lester thought that to mean, and rightly so, that the boy would keep his book and his gun. Still, Lester was uneasy about what had happened. He told his mother he would bury the dog on the riverbank. Maybe high water would wash it downstream but he wasn't going to tell anybody about it. The boy thought that over a lifetime Lester was always burying something.

PART SIX

Religion

THE PROPOSAL

The Reverend Gunder Fagin was a round, soft-looking man, with a mind that was anything but round and soft. As he sat facing Mina, his hands were folded prayerfully before him over an amply bulging waist. He wore a black suit shiny with wear spots, a white shirt, black tie. He was younger than Mina by several years. She was listening carefully to what he said. As she listened, she realized that this man was proposing to her. He was talking about God's intentions for men and women to love and honor each other. He said he know how hard it was for a widow to raise a family alone. He cleared his throat and said he knew, especially, how a small boy needed a father. Especially a boy who needed a name. He was even willing, as an act of Christian charity, to give the boy his name legally if he became his spiritual guardian.

Mina remained silent as he pondered along. She didn't often go to church; but since the boy had been going to Sunday school, she had gone occasionally, especially to the children's Christmas and Easter programs. Now as she listened, she could hear the sermon. The plan for her salvation was being unfolded for her. She would have only to embrace the faith through this man.

There was more. A woman needed a man to give purpose and direction to her life. She had been unfortunate in her behavior. It had been God's will that she was widowed, but it was a man who had made her a grass widow. With him as her protector, she would be safe and secure from any such creatures.

The sounds from the kitchen divided her attention. The boy had come in from outside. She heard him go to the breadbox, open it. She heard the dog's begging whine. Jube wasn't supposed to be in the house. She heard the boy's stifled giggle. She tensed, knowing what was happening. The kitchen with its wide pine flooring had endured thousands of scrubbings. Jube, to his pleasure, had discovered its mild abrasive. Whenever he got in the house he would squat, raise his hind legs and pull himself across the floor with an expression of ecstatic bliss that usually sent the boy into howls of laughter. The stifled giggle was the boy's concession to the minister's presence.

"Honus, take the dog out."

"Yes, Mama."

The screen door slammed. The boy peered around the corner at them. Through a mouthful of biscuit he mumbled,

"He's out, Mama."

"Honus, you know he's not to be in the house."

"Yes, Mama, but it's all right. He didn't have time to get any slivers in his ass. I looked."

Mina pursed her lips, gritted her teeth, sighed a deep sigh.

"Go get stove wood and water,"

"Yes, Mamma." The screen door banged shut and he was gone.

The minister's neck was pink above his white collar.

"The boy needs a man's hand, Mina."

She stood, "He's a good little boy. He'll have to learn to live with his mother's mistake. There will be no more mistakes. He goes to Sunday school. Alice Paulsen is a wonderful teacher."

The minister faced his rejection stiffly, said no more, and departed.

REVEREND FAGIN

Mina arrived as the bell was ringing the call to worship. Honus was waiting for her because he had come earlier to Sunday school. The Paulsen sisters, Marie and Alice, held the classes. Marie, the older, took the older children, mostly girls because the boys were working in the fields in the summer. Alice, with the small ones, was well liked. She told them Bible stories from a Lutheran reprint that depended heavily on the New Testament. The miracles, the Christmas story, the Easter story were read by Alice Paulsen. The stories were told as parables, with the moral explained. Then there was discussion which was mostly the teacher asking questions and the children raising their hands to answer. There were little songs as "Jesus Loves Me," "Jesus Wants Me For a Sunbeam," and activities as learning the Lord's Prayer, the Apostles' Creed, the Twenty-Third Psalm, the Doxology. The children, by and large, were well-behaved, except the Bergsons and the Kassenberg boys who couldn't sit still and who giggled at anything they couldn't understand. Alice's classes were in the back corner of the church. Marie's were at the front. The minister had other churches, so he didn't preach every Sunday. When he was present, he would begin preparing the older children for confirmation.

It was a hot summer morning in late June. The Reverend Gunder Fagin, a short soft man, leaning toward obesity, with short pudgy fingers, well manicured, leafed through the Bible before him on the pulpit. He looked out on the sparsely populated congregation, decimated at harvest time. He saw Mina with the boy sitting beside her. He winced at the memory of his rejection. There was no printed program, so the minister announced the first hymn. Marie Paulsen played accompaniment on the old bellows-type organ while sister Alice, standing beside her, led the congregation in song. Holding the hymnal, the boy stood beside his mother. He followed the words, but mostly he listened to his mother. Mina sang in something approaching a falsetto voice. The boy didn't know that word, but he knew his mother sang in a totally different tone than she talked.

When Fagin stood up in the pulpit to begin his sermon he made some remarks about the weather, thanked the Lord for the incoming harvest, and spoke in glowing terms of the Decoration Day program that he and Miss Foster had worked together to prepare. Then he began his sermon which touched on the ministry years of Jesus. How, even though they were brief, and how in the end he had sacrificed his life to save us all, Jesus himself had been a follower of the law as set down by Moses in the first five books of the Old Testament. Then he went directly to the point.

"When Moses preached the second law to the Israelites, it came down to us as the fourth book of the Old Testament which is Deuteronomy."

Fagin was not a dynamic preacher. Some in the congregation were following along in the Bible. He continued.

"Moses reminded the Israelites about God's rule and law. He did this in sermons. First, life would be different in the promised land from life in the wilderness. However, their God would be the same. Second, he named Joshua as his successor, a reward for his faithfulness. Finally he commended himself to God and died. The Israelites grieved for him for thirty days."

The minister took a deep breath. He raised his voice to an uncharacteristic shout, jolting everyone awake.

"Jesus loved the Book of Deuteronomy. He quoted from it many times. When the devil tempted him three times, he answered each time with a verse from Deutonomy. And when he was asked to name the greatest commandment, he replied by quoting another verse from Deuteronomy, 'You shall love the Lord your God with all your heart, and with all your soul and with all your might.' That comes from Chapter six, Verse five. And as we read on and trust the Lord, more of the words we live by are in Chapter Twenty-three, Verse two: 'No bastard shall enter the assembly of the Lord; even to the tenth generation none of his descendents shall enter the assembly of the Lord.' What I have given you is the word of God. Let us not embrace evil among us. We live with the consequences of our sins. Amen." Stunned silence followed.

"And now will you remember our needs with your offerings. Ushers, please, Mr. Paulsen, Mr. Thomas, please."

The two older men picked up the collection plates atop the organ and began passing along the pews. Mina and Honus were the only ones seated in that row. When Paulsen approached her, he saw an almost imperceptible shake from Mina. He hurried on to the next pew, eyes averted. When the ushers brought the collection plates to the minister, he ascended to the altar and placed them there. Then he turned and brought up his hands in silent command for everyone to stand. The organ began to wheeze out the

Doxology with Alice Paulsen leading off. "Praise God from whom all blessings flow . . ."

The minister, hands clasped behind him, proceeded placidly toward the entry to greet his congregation as they left the church. Most of them shook his hand and left hurriedly. When Mina and the boy reached him she stopped. Her anger was composed. They were the same height, so she looked squarely in his face.

"You blame my boy for something I did." She spoke in an even tone that flustered the minister. His reddening face was aware of the people still standing in line. He was about to speak when Mina continued.

"If God said those things to Moses and Jesus believed what Moses said, then He would send my boy to hell because of me?" She took the boy's hand, she turned away and then turned back.

"My father gave the land for this church and for the graveyard. I'll never come to this church as long as I live. I don't suppose my boy will either, but that's up to him." With that she turned and walked away.

The scene was etched in the boy's memory. They crossed the lawn to the gate, past old man Jensen's grave with the faded flag still standing, and out to the Oakland. She sobbed as they drove away. The boy put his head on her shoulder. Neither spoke.

In the days that followed, there were many things said about what had happened in church that Sunday. However, the minister was on his ground. He had quoted the law right from the Bible. "People have got to obey God's laws, else we'll all roast," was said and repeated. "Preachers are there to remind us what can happen and that's what he did." All in all, the minister had made his point. They didn't like him better for it, but he was a man of the cloth and every word he said was in the Bible. Some had looked it up to know for sure.

During the following week the weather was unsettled. Midweek several twisters set down. They were powerful little tornadoes that could lay down a swath of grain or pick up a straw pile and turn it into whiskers on a fence post. One such followed the section road all the way to the river. Then it veered into the river, sucking up tons of river bottom mud which it carried up the bank and whacked against the side of the church. Some windows were broken, but mostly it was just a muddy mess to clean up. That same afternoon the Ladies Aid Society was holding their monthly meeting at Alvina Bergson's house several miles away. Her husband Goodwin, everybody called him Goodie, was at work in the fields. The minister was always invited to the meeting to give the blessing and to partake of the shared cooking and baking of the potluck meal. He parked his new A-Ford out by the mailbox so as to avoid any blockage. "Last one in, first one out," he said to himself.

The twister had a sound-rush like a train. The ladies, hearing it, scattered themselves around the house. The minister paled and trembled, but continued dishing up the victuals from the potluck meal, determined to show his faith in the Almighty and to satisfy his hunger. The twister funnelled on, staying close to the road. Its vortex settled on the minister's car, which it picked up and carried a quarter mile into Bergson's cornfield. When the ladies reassembled, nervous but unharmed, they found a very disturbed preacher talking to a very agitated farmer who had seen the car ascend and then descend into the cornfield. Towing the car with his tractor, Goodie Bergson lost a few more rows of corn. The car started. The car ran. The minister left. Mostly people laughed.

"Car was on the way to heaven until they found out the preacher wasn't in it," came from Elton Gunderson, an oafish church non-attender.

"Anyone on his way to heaven needs all the help he can get," said old man Tilsen, who wasn't one of the faithful either.

Mina thought to herself, "Serves him right," but she wasn't ready for what she heard when it got back that maybe the boy had something to do with the mud-spotted church and the preacher's car. Lester had heard it too. When they talked about it, Mina said,

"If they think a little boy could have anything to do with something like that, let 'em think so, let 'em stew." That was the end of it.

PART SEVEN

Humor

GOOSEBERRY JELLY, CHOKECHERRY JAM

Mason jars lined the shelves along the walls of the basement. By the end of harvest season the shelves were filled with jars of vegetables, fruit, and meat waiting for winter. By spring the same jars, empty, awaited the next canning season.

"If it grows under the ground," Mina said, "It will keep in the root cellar." She canned corn, peas and green beans suspiciously. "If they spoil in the jar they'll kill you," she said.

Fruit. She canned fruit enthusiastically; plums, rhubarb, campos cherries were favorites. Apples went into the root cellar with the underground vegetables and potatoes. Jars were not wasted on anything that had a storage life of its own. The kitchen garden was generous all summer long. Always by the Fourth of July there were fresh green peas and new potatoes for supper.

By midsummer the woods yielded their bounty. Honus learned about picking gooseberries from Mina. They were everywhere along the river bank. Not quite that simple. There were nettles that stung, poison ivy to avoid, cockleburrs that stuck and refused to leave. Wild gooseberries are small and green with white stripes. They look like a tiny melon. They grow on thorny branches and are stripped branch by branch. Honus learned to strip them into a small Karo syrup bucket. It took many buckets to make a batch of Mina's gooseberry jelly. Honus always wondered why little green berries made such bright red jelly. It only happened after stemming, boiling, and straining and whatever else Mina did before they reached a jelly jar.

Lester had always picked chokecherries for Mina. Honus inherited the task with Lester's help. Chokecherries grow on thin supple-trunked trees. Lester could reach the lower branches. Honus could climb to the tops of the trees. Chokecherries were elegant, glistening, garnet-shaded beads of fruit, both sweet and tart, perfect for jam, also tempting while picking. Honus climbed and picked, picked and climbed. Mina couldn't believe the amount he brought home.

Honus didn't connect his stomach ache that night with the taste of chokecherries, but it wasn't long before Mina did. The backhouse was too far away for use at night. Under the bed was the thing known to Honus only as the piss pot. Mina hustled him out of bed just in time. The explosion sounded like a hailstorm. When Mina cleaned the pot next morning, she found the cause.

"Honus, those are chokecherry pits."

Lester howled with laughter, "He sat up there in the tree and ate 'em seeds and all."

Honus hung his head, "Nobody told me not to."

Mina shook her head, sighed, and left.

Lester laughed, "You dumb shit. You know better now, don't you?"

Mina made wonderful chokecherry jam.

ACRONYMS

The January morning was crisp, cold, and clear. Lester and Honus were already seated at table.

"It's a hot meal morning, boys," said Mina, "graveyard stew."

Graveyard stew—bread chunked and toasted in the oven, sprinkled with cinnamon and raisins, soaked in scalding milk. She set bowls full before her boys. Then she served herself.

The night before had combined snow and cold with a full moon and northern lights to create an eerie lucent landscape. The lights had been the brightest they had ever seen. The boys dug into their breakfast, they talked between mouthfuls. Mina listened. Lester was explaining that the sun reflected its light off the icebergs at the North Pole.

"They're really big icebergs and when the wind blows them around, the lights go away up." It was the explanation he had been given all his life.

Honus was skeptical, "How come they don't look like a rainbow?"

"How should I know?" snorted an exasperated Lester. "I suppose you know where all those colors come from."

The boy was thoughtful. "Well, my book says—"

Lester rolled his eyes up into his head. "The book again," he said.

Honus continued, "It's called a prism effect. When the sun shines through rain the rays separate out into seven colors."

Lester squinted, "How do you know seven?" he asked.

"Well, my book says—"

Lester grunted, "Ugh, that book again." "V.I.B.G.Y.O.R.," said Honus. "What're you talkin' about, boy!" exclaimed Lester.

Honus grinned, "It's called an acronym. The first letter of each color helps you remember it." He held up his fingers, "Violet, Indigo, Blue, Green, Yellow, Orange, Red, V.I.B.G.Y.O.R."

Mina smiled and shook her head, "Well, I learned something, Lester. I always thought rainbows were pretty. Guess now I know why. Get a move on, boys; Honus, bundle up, time for school. Lester," she grinned, "Now you know the difference between an iceberg and a rainbow."

THE HARMONICA

Stubby's four-cornered neckerchief was all he ever traveled with. It was knotted and hung over his shoulder on a stick. Every thing he owned was in it. When Honus saw him digging into it, he was curious.

"Lookin' for?" he asked.

Stubby produced a small box.

"Harmonica," he said, "Only I call it a mouth organ."

He cupped it in his hands, over his mouth. He blew out and in a couple of times, then played "Home, Sweet Home." For the boy it was a new and unique experience. Stubby, his eyes closed, played on. He played what the boy would later know as Stephen Foster songs: "Old Black Joe," ""Darlin' Nellie Gray," "My Ol' Kentucky Home." Mina came from the kitchen to listen; Jube came out from under the porch. Soon Jube started his hound dog bay. Honus, listening to Stubby and watching Jube, was laughing uproariously. When Stubby stopped, Jube stopped.

"He don't know the words, and he can't carry a tune any better'n I can, can you Jube?" Jube wagged his answer.

Mina was wiping her hands on her apron. "Must be that those sounds hurt his ears; that makes him howl."

"Does it hurt your ears too, boy?"

In answer, Honus asked for more. He also wanted to know the words to the music. Stubby knew them from memory.

"Old Black Joe," he said, "the words are like a poem.

> Gone are the days when my heart was young and gay.
> Gone are my friends from the cotton fields away
> Gone from the earth to a better land I know.
> I hear their gentle voices calling, Old Black Joe."

Up to then, black was only a word and a color to Honus. Now he learned about slavery from Stubby. Honus memorized the words, so when Stubby played the tune he sang them while Jube howled out his pain. Mina smiled; Stubby was barely able to keep his mind on the tune.

Finally Stubby said, "That's enough for one day."

Honus asked if he could try to play the mouth organ. Stubby shook his head.

"Never play somebody else's instrument. They don't want your germs." "Besides," he grinned, "see this sore on my lip, you don't want it." Stubby boxed his harmonica.

As he stood to leave, Mina said, "Ear wax."

Stubby, brow furrowed, repeated "Ear wax?"

"Yes," said Mina, "Dig some wax out of your ear and rub it on your sore lip. It'll be gone tomorrow.

When Stubby returned from town on Sunday, he handed Honus a package.

Honus squealed, "Mama, look what Stubby got me!"

Stubby, straight faced, said, "It's a Hohner, key of C, the best there is. Don't let anybody else play it, and wash out your mouth before you play it yourself."

As Stubby was leaving, Mina said, "I'd like to pay you for that."

Stubby grinned, "No, ma'am, not often you can bring somebody that much fun. Besides, I owe you. That ear wax really works."

PART EIGHT

Tragedies

CRAZY KARL

Karl Stensholm got himself known as "Crazy Karl" because of the way he acted when he was drunk. The name stuck because he was always drunk. The Stensholms had farmed a half-section of good land. When Mrs. Stensholm died, she left three children, Karl, Ella and Dina, and her husband, feeble Old Man Stensholm. The girls took care of him until he died not long after his wife. Stensholm had willed the land to his son, and his savings to the girls, who left the farm and promised each other and Karl that they would look after him. They moved to town and looked for work. They could sew and cook, were marriageable maybe. In fact, eventually both did marry. The girls tried to care for Karl but found it both hopeless and thankless. But Karl alone couldn't cope. He ended up renting his land to the Dirksons. They sharecropped it half and half. The sisters came every week with groceries, mostly tinned meat and beans. They never saw Karl sober or civil. Their stays were brief. Karl spent his days sitting on an old platform rocker on the porch.

Stubby, the boy and Jube rambled through the woods, following the river's bends, past the Tedemans, the Pearsons, the Tilsens, avoiding nettles, picking up cockleburrs, stalking squirrels, woodchucks, rabbits, anything that moved. Carrying his .22, the boy followed Jube. Stubby stayed back out of harm's way. When they came to the old Stensholm place there was a fence all the way to the river's edge with an opening on higher ground. The boy whistled to Jube and they headed for the opening. They cut across the front of the old house.

When Jube and the boy and Stubby came across the yard, Karl was dozing in his rocking chair. He had his father's old ten-gauge shotgun propped beside him. Some sound or movement aroused him. He saw the boy first, then Jube. He was a fearful sight with scraggly beard, a wall eye, grimy underwear, bib overalls, homespun stockings, shoeless.

He roared at the boy, "That's my dog! Where the hell did you get him?" Then he squinted. "You're Mina's little bastard boy, aren't you?"

Not waiting for a response, Karl reached for the shotgun. Jube, who knew no fear, faced him from twenty feet with his back hair up, growling teeth bared. The boy's shriek was in two words—"Jube, git!"

A ten gauge double barreled shotgun is a small cannon. Karl swung it around toward Jube. Stubby, standing unnoticed, said,

"Don't shoot!"

Karl in his drunken stupor turned, startled. The gun was a foot from his shoulder when he squeezed the trigger. The recoil twisted him and drove him over the porch rail. The open cellar door below the porch made a drop of six feet under the house. The roar of the explosion sent man, boy and dog running. They hid by the riverbank until Stubby said,

"Let me go look."

The porch rail was splintered. The gaping cellar door stood open. Karl was lying with his feet on the stairs, his body at an odd angle on the cellar floor. Stubby closed the cellar door. When he returned to Jube and the boy he said, "Let's not talk about this with anybody."

When Karl's sisters came with groceries, they didn't find him. They stopped at the Dirkson's on their way home. Not really worried, they asked if Ada or her men had seen him. Negative. The sisters then drove back to town. Ada went by during the following week. She noticed the groceries had not been touched, and wondered. When she called Dina in town and told her about the groceries, the girls decided to come out the next day.

The groceries were still where they had set them. As they passed the cellar door there was a noticeable stench. When Ella raised one side of the cellar door, she saw Karl's feet on the stairway. Her gasp was both for air and from hysteria. Ella and Dina drove to the Dirkson farm and called the sheriff from there.

The sheriff, Charley Peterson, was a stocky man in his fifties going toward fat. He didn't know the Stensholm sisters when they called him, but he knew Crazy Karl. He had sobered Karl up in jail some years back and had dragged him out of a Front Street whorehouse when his folks were still living. He told the sisters he would investigate. Not to worry. He would get right on it.

Peterson's deputy was his sister's boy, his namesake, Charley Sorenson. He picked him up on the way out of town.

"Sounds like old Crazy Karl's done in."

"Could be so. Not much lost, but we better look first."

On the way to the old Stensholm farm they drove by the Dirkson brothers working in the field. When Sheriff Peterson lifted the cellar door he was looking at the most distasteful job he had ever had to face. He turned to young Sorenson.

"Get over to the Dirkson place and call Doc Winters. We'll need a coroner's report on this one."

Doc Winters came with the Smith Brothers undertakers dray. Winters put a bandanna over his face when he went down in the cellar. Karl's face was pretty much gone. Rats had eaten the soft tissue around his nose, cheeks and mouth. His eyes were only sockets and any exposed tissue was swarming with maggots. Without touching anything the doctor's first observation was,

"Broken neck. Looks like he died where he's laying."

"Gun's laying alongside him," said the sheriff Peterson.

He took out a handkerchief and picked up the shotgun, cracked it and saw that both shells had been fired.

"Suicide?"

Winters shook his head. "There wouldn't be this much left with that monster. More than likely he was pointing it at somebody or something else."

The sheriff asked, "Any reason we can't take him out now?"

"Can't see why not."

Peterson sent his deputy out to the field to get the Dirksons. When they returned he told them about Karl in the cellar.

"I'm deputizing you two. Together we'll get what's down here into the undertaker's wagon."

Very reluctantly the Dirksons helped get Karl's body onto a litter and into the hearse. The coroner headed for town. The Dirksons wasted no time getting away, and the sheriff and young Sorenson started making their report.

"Smells funny in more ways than one," said Sheriff Peterson. "That cellar door was closed when his sisters found him. Somebody closed it. Karl had a broken neck, so he sure as hell didn't get up and close it."

Sorenson had gone into the house. "Groceries still sitting on the table from a week ago; the place is filthy, but no evidence of a struggle."

The sheriff pointed to the broken porch rail. "Could be that's got something to do with it."

They went down in the cellar. There were straw bales piled up to the rafters across most of the cellar. The sheriff scratched his head.

"Why in the hell would anybody bring all that straw into a cellar?"

He looked, kicked it, but it didn't budge. He pulled off the top bale and saw shiny metal behind it. Pulling off more bales he found neatly stacked five-gallon tins.

"Holy shit, if this is what I think it is, we've found us a drop house."

Young Sorenson looked on in wide-eyed amazement. The sheriff lifted down a five-gallon tin, unscrewed the lid, stuck his finger in the screwtop and put it to his lips.

"Pure alky, I'll be a son-of-a-bitch, no wonder Karl was always drunk." Before he said any more he took down another tin.

"I think we better keep these for evidence," he said to his deputy. "And we'd better get the Feds going on the rest of it. Put these in the trunk of my car. You stand by here 'til I bring the Feds."

With the tins stored in the trunk, Sheriff Peterson told his deputy to hide out where he could see the cellar door and just keep an eye open.

"Don't interfere with anybody, just watch."

When the sheriff returned, there was a small army of G-men with him. It was their job to smell out these drop houses from the Canadian border to Chicago. There was a fortune in uncut alcohol in old Karl's cellar. They took the tins out and punctured them, every one of them. A match would have turned that old yard into a blue blaze.

After the Feds finished their task, they congratulated Peterson and his deputy, thanked him, and sent them on his way. Headed back to town, he winked at young Sorenson.

"We still have the evidence we collected. Let's just keep it to ourselves for now. It may come in handy."

Karl Stensholm was buried in the family plot beside his parents. An old Scandinavian custom was observed when the farmers got together after the funeral. The women brought potluck dishes and the men were served a drink from jugs at the door. The sheriff saw to it that nobody got drunk. He also saw to it that every man had a drink. He listened to them talk. Although the alky loosened tongues, there was nothing said about the closed cellar door. In the dining room he came upon a teary-eyed Ada.

"I tried to keep track of Karl," she said, "Went over there and checked ever so often."

The sheriff asked, "Did you ever notice that cellar door being open?"

Ada looked at him, "I closed it any number of times. Can't tell you how many."

"Recently, did you?"

"I could have, it's hard to say."

"If I write what you just said, would you sign a statement?"

"Well, yes, I guess, it's the truth."

"Ma'am, you not only closed the cellar door, you closed the case. I'm much obliged."

The coroner's report read that Karl Stensholm died from a broken neck probably caused by a fall from his porch. Bruises on his shoulder were probably caused by the recoil of his shotgun, which he had discharged for reasons unknown. The splintered porch rail could indicate that he fell through it and into the cellar.

The sheriff's report was much shorter: "Accidental death resulted from a fall per the coroner's report. Mrs. Dirkson's statement is attached that she had closed the cellar door on numerous occasions and did so without noticing the body on this occasion. Case closed."

HAILSTORM

Morning chores were done, breakfast over. The day's work ahead was getting ready for potato picking. Lester was working on the potato digger, adjusting and sharpening the little spades that dig down beneath the potato hills and dig up the potatoes. Stubby and Honus were sorting burlap sacks. The older sacks had seen duty and some were no longer usable; so there would be new ones to buy. They worked in the cave-like coolness of the root cellar, the entrance facing toward the afternoon sun. Slowly they became aware that the dimness around them was because of a boiling mass of clouds to the west. They stood at the cellar entrance in wonder.

"Jesus, look at the colors," exclaimed Stubby.

Backlit by the obscured sun, the clouds were an iridescent green; flecks of lightning threaded through the rolling nimbus clouds. Mina had seen it too. She called to Lester in the machine shed and to Stubby and Honus.

"Get in the house. It could be a hailstorm."

The livestock had shelters, but the barn door to the pasture had been left open for the only team of horses still on the farm. Max and Maude had been on the farm for years. They were used during winter to pull an old stone-boat when the snow was too deep for a tractor. They were an inseparable team because Maude was blind in one eye. Max led her on her blind side whenever they were in harness. He also seemed to sense her needs and would guide her from the pasture into the barn and into her stall. Hearing the crackle of thunder and lightning from the approaching storm, Maude panicked and ran from the barn into the pasture.

Lester and Mina, Stubby and Honus all gathered in the house on the screened front porch. The huge emerald curtain moved inexorably toward them. The first wave covered the ground white with buckshot pellets of ice that quickly began to melt into the warm earth. They also stung poor old Maude's flanks. She began running her one-eyed pattern, circling and circling the pasture. The hail began again, marble-sized, minie ball-shaped. Stubby stood up.

"That poor old spooked horse has gotta get into the barn."

He went to the screen door. He turned to Honus, held up his hand and squeezed his thumb and forefinger, smiled his crooked grin, and ran into the hailstorm. He covered the ground to the barn with his loping gait. Once there, he bridled Max and led him out the door to the pasture. He ran with Max to Maude's blind side and yelled into Max's ear,

"Take her to the barn."

He slapped Max's rump as the hailstones increased in size. The only shelter in the pasture was an ancient elm, a reminder of homestead days. Stubby ran to the shelter of the elm. The fury now descended. Huge fist-shaped chunks of ice were hurled with shotgun velocity; the crash of glass, the crunch of shingles, the snap of breaking branches landing on the ground the thump of a sledge hammer. The soft earth held them until they were shattered by another deluge. Lightning and thunder were continuous.

Honus watched Stubby hug the old elm. Then a huge pillar of fire seemed to reach from the tree skyward. From above, a rope of light descended. The sound and the light were one. Mina and Lester were dazed and blinded. Honus, curled in a ball, unwound and peered through the screen. The elm was split from top to bottom, laid open like a banana peel. Stubby was standing amidst the foliage. Honus saw him beckon, ran across the yard and squeezed between the barbed wire strands. He ran to the elm where he embraced what remained of Stubby. Stubby's head had exploded from the lightning bolt, his body was blackened, his clothing in shreds.

When Mina saw the boy running across the yard she screamed and scrambled to her feet. Lester held her.

"Don't, for God's sake, don't."

They clung to each other. Honus had run from the house to the elm untouched. His trail through the hail was visible. Then the storm left as quickly as it came.

When Mina and Lester reached the boy he was clinging to Stubby. No tears, an icy calm.

"Why did you do that, Honus?" Mina asked.

"Stubby waved me to come," said Honus.

Lester snorted, "He was dumb to go out in the first place. Then he gets killed, and then he waves to you. Shit, Hon, you're talking crazy."

"Stubby's dead, I saw his ghost. Nobody else could see it but me."

Poor Mina, shocked to numbness by what had happened, now began to function.

"Get Stubby to the cellar," she ordered.

Lester carried what was left of Stubby to the basement; laid him on the old carving table. Mina looked on, wondering where to start.

"Lester, we've got to do this," she said, as she put on an old butcher apron. She sent Lester for a bucket of water; Honus she sent to the bunkhouse to get Stubby's change of clothes. She forced herself to examine Stubby's blackened body. She peeled away tatters of cloth that were cooked into skin and flesh. His feet had grounded the huge lightning bolt. Headless and footless, Stubby's crumpled corpse was not much to prepare. When Mina uncovered his torso she gasped. His groin and genitals were covered with warts, now dried and blackened like the sole of a boot. Her memory flashed back to his shame when Minnick had ridiculed him.

She dressed him as best she could. With Lester she measured the size needed to make a coffin for Stubby. Pine boards used to separate bins were stacked in the granary. Lester cut and cornered the end and sides, made a bottom and a lid. He put it on the truck bed of the Reo and drove to the house. Mina was quick with praise.

"A carpenter couldn't do better, Lester."

Daylight was gone now. There was still much to do. Lester was pleased and proud of his mother's praise, but dismayed at her next direction.

"The trunk in the attic. The one with the quilts. Bring one."

Lester was appalled. "Grandma's quilts? Why?"

"It's to line the coffin, Lester," she said.

"Can't we just use gunny sacks?" he pleaded.

Mina's lips were a thin straight line. "Lester, just do it."

Lester sorted through the quilts, found the one most faded and timeworn. He muttered to himself about the wastefulness of it all. Mina lined the coffin with her mother's wedding ring quilt. Together they gingerly put Stubby's remains in it and nailed down the lid.

Lester took a deep breath. "Now what?"

Mina wiped her brow and answered Lester, "Put it on the truck," pointing to the coffin. "Take it over to the churchyard. Park out by the old livery stable. Take a spade and dig way back by the back fence. Cut the sod out in chunks and dig down to clay. Bury him, and cover it over and put the sod back in place. Spread the extra around. Then come home, son. Will you do that?"

"Yes, Mama."

Honus watched, listened, didn't ask; and wasn't told.

In the darkness Lester returned, bone-weary, sweat-stained. Mina had supper on the table for him by the time he had washed up. He ate in silence. Mina sat with him. Honus was asleep.

"It's been a day," she said.

Lester took a deep breath, "Tomorrow we'll have to patch up the roofs and clean up after the storm. It didn't hurt the potatoes much, being still under ground."

Mina tried a smile, "You did a man's job today, son, get some sleep."

Shattered shingles, broken windows, the debris of broken tree limbs, downed trees and flattened corn were more than a day's work. Lester and the boy began with the elm tree. The old patriarch of the pasture was a big tree. They cut away the foliage first. Then, while Lester sawed up the trunk, Honus pulled the branches to the riverbank. Mina drove to the lumber yard at the railroad track for shingles and pane glass. One of Osbert Lange's boys loaded the bundles of shingles and cut the glass panes for her.

"Hailstorm do your crop damage?" he asked.

"Enough. Took most of the corn, but the spuds are still in the ground."

Lange looked at the shingles. Mina shook her head.

"I may be back for more. The barn roof is in bad shape."

When she got back to the farm, the old elm was only a stump. It left a gaping hole that seemed to open across to the horizon. The emptiness brought tears. The old elm went all the way back to her childhood.

Calling Honus, she sent him to the garden.

"Pull up what you can find," she said.

She had stopped at the creamery on the way home and brought meat from the freezer locker. When the boy came back with carrots and turnips and beets, she asked about the garden. Honus told her.

"Lettuce, cabbage, stringbeans, sweet corn are gone."

Mina sighed, "Go get some potatoes, it looks like we are going to be eating lots of potatoes for a while."

Mina made a pot of stew for dinner and supper too. Lester worked through the afternoon shingling and replacing windowpanes. Mina cleaned up the cellar and then sat down on the front porch. Finally overcome, she sat alone and cried.

When Lester came, Mina was in the kitchen heating supper. Lester looked around.

"Where's Honus?"

"Wasn't he with you?"

"Haven't seen him all afternoon."

"Where can he be? Where would he go?" they asked each other.

They searched the house room by room to no avail. Standing in his room, Mina looked at the wall over his bed where there were two nails side by side.

"His medal—it's gone! Lester, get the truck."

Lester was puzzled. "Where to?"

"The churchyard."

After dinner Honus and Jubilo had gone down to the riverbank. They found shade although Jube wanted some action. Honus broke a stick and threw it in the river. Jube dove after it. When he recovered the stick, the current had carried him downstream to where he could crawl out of the water. After a tug-of-war the boy tossed the stick again and again Jube returned it. The third time, Jube stood on the bank and watched the stick drift away. Jube had made Honus smile. A wag and a bark acknowledged the smile.

An idea had been shaping in the boy's mind. He went back to the house and took down Roald Jensen's medal from above his bed. Then he and Jube followed the river to the bridge by the church. The afternoon sun was losing its heat when they entered the churchyard. They passed Jensen's grave and went on to where Honus could see the sod had been tamped in place. He laid the medal on Stubby's grave.

"Mr. Jensen knows why I'm doing this, Stubby. He knows what you did to save old Maude. You're both here now. I'll never forget."

Jube watched the boy, ears cocked, as Honus talked. The boy sat cross-legged by the grave. Jube stood listening.

"Is he saying good-bye, Jube? Can you hear him?" Jube sat back on his haunches and made whining sounds. There was a boy, a dog, and a presence.

Mina and Lester arrived at the churchyard at dusk. They could barely make out the two small figures at the back of the graveyard. They made their way to Honus and Jube.

Mina said gently, "You didn't tell us."

"I didn't think, Mama. I just did it."

It rang in Mina's ear—"Just do it." She had said it only yesterday.

"Let's go home, Hon."

The boy got to his feet. Mina took his hand.

"Lester, bring Jubilo along. He can ride on the back of the truck."

She and Honus climbed into the Reo. When Lester came, he put Jubilo on the truckbed and they headed for home.

Busy weeks followed the storm. The hired potato pickers brought in a good crop. Sorted, graded and sacked, the potatoes were loaded on the Speedwagon and taken to the railroad loading platform in Oakville.

Mr. Hagen, the potato broker, supervised the loading as he had in years past. Mina had trusted him since she had gone to him for advice the years after Jacob's death. Hagen had enjoyed outguessing the weather and the market.

He admired Mina for the way she ran her farm and raised her boys. A grass widow had a hard row to hoe. Besides, she was German, as was Hagen.

With the crops in and an early frost, Mina and Lester closed the books on the year's crops. In spite of tragedy and hail damage, it was much more than a "make do" year.

Lester made the suggestion. Mina was both surprised and pleased. He wanted to take Honus on a fishing trip. Where? Maybe Bemidji. Maybe Leech Lake. The next day Lester went to town. That evening he was assembling gear when Honus came into the kitchen.

"Doin'?" he asked.

Lester handed him a spool of line and told him to hold it. "This is a level wind reel. The best."

Honus looked on. "You going fishing, Lester?" he asked.

"Think so, yeah, think so."

"Where?"

"Big lakes, maybe Leech Lake," said Lester.

The boy looked longingly at the new rod and reel. "When you going?"

"Depends," said Lester.

"Well, your rig's ready," said Honus.

Lester just looked at him. "Oh, that's not my rig."

"Whose it is?"

Lester grinned, "Yours."

They had a week of living in a lodge run by a French Indian and his squaw. They fished in the early morning and at sunset. Lester fished with lures. Plugs he called them. The boy fished with minnows. Lester stood in the prow and cast into the shallow wild rice beds. He filled a stringer of big northern pike. Honus fished over the side of the boat. He brought in walleyes. The Indian squaw cleaned all their catch, but she fried the walleyes in bacon grease for their dinners.

"Snow white meat," she said, "Best." She also cooked fried potatoes, gamy venison stew and wild rice.

The French Indian called himself Beauchamp. He took them back to swamps covered with low bush cranberries and swales of hazelnut bushes. By week's end, cranberries and hazelnuts and a case of iced fish filled the back seat and the trunk. Lester drove. Honus slept all the way home. It was a complete and total experience, a lifetime in a week.

MAUDE

One corner of the machine shed was railed off. The boy's earliest memories of it were clear and vivid. Long unused, it was covered with dust. By Honus's time a one-horse sleigh was no more than a showpiece. Honus had asked Lester about it, but he too knew little; and since it had no moving parts it held little interest for him.

Honus found that when Mina was ironing clothes she would talk about things in the past. Ironing was a mindless task, so the boy's company and his everlasting curiosity amused her. Honus would sit on a stool opposite the ironing board in the kitchen near the stove. One of the sadirons was heating on the stove while the other was in use. Mina ironed everything that wrinkled. That included just about everything: shirts, overalls, dresses, even bedsheets. Lester's big red handkerchiefs and work socks were pressed and neatly folded. The heat and monotony of her task gave Honus his chance for questions. When he first asked about the sleigh, Mina was hesitant, even reluctant to answer his questions. Did she ever ride in it? Did she ever drive it? Why was it just sitting in the machine shed? Slowly the cross-examination turned toward confession.

She told him about her father. She referred to him as "Vater," the German way. She remembered riding in the sleigh before there were cars, at a time when Maude was a high-stepping, spirited young horse who could pull those slim runners through the snow with great pureness and speed. Her father, Charles, had gone skimming up the road, a small bearded creature swelled and glowing with pride. He visited his neighbors in the winter when few ventured out. He was known for his kindness and willingness to help. To her he was a stern man who must be obeyed, who seldom smiled at home but was jovial and friendly with his neighbors. Honus learned about him bit by bit. How he came to the Red River valley, built a sod house, brought his family from Wisconsin. Sometimes Mina didn't answer his questions. She had had only three years of schooling and then she had gone to work on the farm, but there was richness in her childhood experiences. Honus looked forward to ironing days, days that were an indelible part of his childhood.

When Maude no longer pulled the sleigh she was teamed with Max. Her eye became sightless, "milked over," an opaque lens that further limited her usefulness, a high-spirited horse that had lost her proud place. Max and his patient plodding way gave her some acceptance. They pulled the stoneboat through the winter snow and earned their keep. The elegant sleigh was stored in the machine shed. The elegant horse grew old in the stable.

On the day that Stubby sent Max out to rescue her from the hailstorm, he spent his life to save her. After that day Maude was never quite the same. She was skittish and nervous and Max's steadiness couldn't seem to calm her. The team was hard to handle. Spring came and with snowmelt the river began to rise. Lester led Maude down by the river bank and stepped back from where she stood. He shot her. She fell by the bank and the rising water carried her downstream the next day.

GRASSHOPPERS

Like flies, ants, and potato bugs, grasshoppers were a part of life. There were mosquitoes and gnats as well that sucked blood or flew into breathing nostrils. Grasshoppers grew big. Walking across a field they were an uninvited escort. Flying into you, they left a stinging impact and a "tobacco juice" discharge.

Honus learned as a small boy that pinching the lower joint of a grasshopper's leg made it kick and the leg would fly off. He also learned early that ants would feast on the carcass of a grasshopper. He would tear off wings and legs and drop the squirming doomed creature onto an anthill and watch the ants devour the hapless creature down to its skeletal husk. From Lester he learned how to hook grasshoppers to catch bullheads and catfish in the river.

People said that when conditions were right, climate, moisture, the hatching year, there would be a plague of grasshoppers. When it came, even those who predicted it were left to wonder at its intensity.

The grasshoppers came from the Dakotas in such swarms that they darkened the sun. They ate every kind of fiber: grain heads, stalks, vines, tree leaves, small branches. They gnawed at fence posts. They ate clothes on a clothesline, then the clothespins, then the clothesline itself. They denuded birch and willow trees of their very bark.

The measures taken to stop them were as drastic as the plague itself. Lester brought a load of bait from town. The bed of the Reo Speedwagon was filled with a sticky mix of sawdust, sugar water, and paris green. He piled cushions on the seat of the truck and hoisted Honus into the driver's seat. He set the hand throttle at its lowest and put it in gear. The truck crawled along at two miles an hour with Honus steering and Lester shoveling the bait from the back of the truck. When the truck was empty, Lester signaled and Honus cut he throttle. They had spread a ton of bait.

The hoppers ate the bait as greedily as they devoured everything else. Then they began flying blindly to their doom. They filled ditches, piled against trees and buildings, stacked like drifted snow against snow fences. The great reeking mass of death took with it both sides of the food chain: bugs, beetles, and insects also died along with birds, gophers, and small creatures of the field. The battlefield was plowed into a cemetery for the millions. For the farmers it was a time to start over.

HYDROPHOBIA

In the sun-drenched morning Jube and the boy walked the riverbank. Heat was already beginning to wilt the broad leaves of ground-covering plants. Only the nettles stood erect, attentive to sting anyone who passed. The boy and the dog skirted them carefully. When they came around the river bend, the burrow of the woodchuck was visible below them. The old marmot lay stretched across his diggings in the hot morning sun. Jube tensed. Both sight and smell had signaled him. He moved soundlessly toward the old chuck. Perhaps his laziness or lack of alertness should have been a danger signal, but to Jube there was only an enemy to kill. The boy could have easily shot the woodchuck from where he stood, but he watched fascinated as Jube skirted a willow thicket and glided noiselessly down toward the burrow. He struck with the deep growling fury of his terrier ancestry, grabbing the torpid old creature by the nape of the neck and shaking him furiously. The woodchuck somehow squirmed under his loose-skinned mane just enough to take a swipe at Jube, catching his upper lip just momentarily and drawing blood. Jube's release was a lightning movement that re-attached behind the woodchuck's ears. With a vicious twist the terrier cracked his spine and tossed him away from the burrow. Jube pounced again and grabbed the quivering woodchuck by the middle of his backbone and shook him until no life remained. Jube offered no opposition when the boy pulled the carcass to the burrow and stuffed it into the grave of its own making. He pushed dirt into the hole and stamped it with his bare feet while Jube looked on.

Along the riverbank there were gooseberries and chokecherries. They crouched in the shade, the two hunters glorying in their deed, neither knowing that the dead woodchuck would break their mortal link and that life would never again be quite as beautiful as that quiet moment on a warm morning at the end of a life.

It was later that Jube began to act strangely. It was as though he had blind staggers and it was funny to watch. The boy laughed at him but finally walked very slowly and coaxed him along. He curled up in the shade next to the house and there he seemed to sleep.

When the men came in from the fields, the boy went out to meet them. Lester was covered with the thick dust of a day on the tractor. He filled the wash basin from a bucket and turned it almost immediately into mud as he immersed his face and hands in it. The boy watched this operation impassively. It took several basins of water before a degree of cleanliness was reached. Jube was still sleeping in the shade when the boy approached him. He was greeted with a growl rather than a wagging tail. There were flecks of foam around Jube's jaws and the boy backed away as Jube tottered to his feet. The two great good friends faced each other in wonderment and fear.

Lester saw what was happening and shouted to the boy to run to the porch. Jube was snarling at his heels as he reached the steps. The boy climbed the rail of the porch with Jube's bare teeth snapping close behind. Lester came out of the screen door loading a shotgun. The boy screamed, "Lester, don't!" Jube lunged toward the boy and met the full charge of the twelve-gauge in mid-air. He seemed to dissolve into a crimson spray of blood and gore. The sobbing boy collapsed into Lester's arms. Lester carried him into the house and laid him on the sofa. It was an hour before he moved.

Jube's body had been dragged to the manure pile behind the barn. It was covered with dung but clouds of flies hovered over the fresh blood that had oozed through manure and straw. The boy took all this in and then went back to the house. The flies hummed thick and black as he made his way into the kitchen. The brother he worshipped most in all the world had just killed his best friend. How he hated the flies for their wicked feast.

The chill of an Indian summer comes in the early morning. Small creatures and vermin that thrive in the summer sun are near the ending of their lives. Bluebottles swarmed toward the light and heat of the kitchen screen door. There they clustered so thick that no light showed through. Honus with a newspaper and match in hand went out by way of the basement door, so as not to disturb them. As the lighted match touched the paper, it flared. Wings were momentarily torches, bodies fell in a squirming heap. When the paper had burned down to his hand the screen door was clear of flies. With a broom and pan he swept the writhing mass into a bucket; at the riverbank he dumped it. In moments there was a feeding frenzy of catfish and bullheads swirling and feasting.

Jube's end was not in the manure pile. Honus opened up an old badger burrow in a far corner of the pasture. He arranged Jube's remains on a gunny sack and carefully carried them to his grave. Stubby and Jube, both torn apart in their deaths, would be the mesh that held the boy's life together in the years that followed.

"Goodbye, Jube," and the tears came. He found a weathered shingle, scratched "Jubilo" on it, and staked it in the mound of earth.

PART NINE

Departure

HAVING AND LEAVING

Lester grew into a big man, not as tall as his father had been, but broad and muscular. He was handsome too, in a raw-boned strong silent way. It was Mina's farm, but by the time Lester was twenty he was running it. Mina paid him the high compliment, "Lester, you're a good farmer." There had been bad years with grasshoppers and crop damage, but mostly good years. Mina was not as quick to change as Lester. When she was getting ready for the threshing crew, Lester had said, "This should be the last year for that." Mina knew what he meant.

"Combines can do the work of a whole crew with only a couple men."

"Lester, they cost too much," was Mina's answer.

"Why should you cook for a whole crew and pay them if you don't have to? Think, mama, how much easier it would be," Lester argued.

"We'll see after harvest." Mina was really giving in. Also, as Lester suggested, she hired a girl to help.

Maybelle Ness had finished Normal School and would be a teacher in the fall when school started. When Mina hired her, she wondered if she would be up to the hard work of serving a threshing crew.

"Long days, from sun-up to clean-up," Mina told her.

"I made it through school. I can sure do kitchen work" Maybelle laughed. She's a smart alec, Mina thought, "We'll see."

As it turned out, she was willing enough but had to be told everything. One thing she did well was serving the crew their meals. She was a born flirt; and she had her eye on Lester. At night Mina found herself cleaning up without help. She found Maybelle sitting on the porch with Lester. Reluctantly, Maybelle followed her reluctantly to the kitchen and was told, "This is your job, do it." Later Mina returned to find Lester, dish towel in hand, helping.

When Mina talked to Lester, she said, "You work all day long in the field, you don't need to work in the kitchen."

Lester, stubborn and blushing, said, "She's not a farm girl. She's nice to talk to."

Harvest ended; Maybelle moved back to town. Lester was seeing her whenever he could. The old Oakland was replaced by a Graham-Paige roadster. "Cash money," Mina had said when they bought it. It was paid for when Lester drove it from the agency. But the combine would not be bought for cash. When Lester went to the bank, Lundeen was still the owner but now had a manager who dealt with customers. A Dutchman like old Lundeen, Mr. Jansen, explained credit and interest to Lester. When Jansen was through, Mr. Lundeen called Lester into his office.

"I recognized your name, Mr. Sorby. Your grandfather, Charles, was my good friend and good customer."

When Mr. Lundeen discussed the possible loan with Lester, he mentioned, "Your mother has never come to the bank for money," he smiled, "except to deposit and withdraw. There aren't too many like her."

Lester spoke with pride of Mina, "Mama doesn't believe in borrowing, but the days of threshing crews are all but gone."

"And you want to combine, do you? Little or big?"

"Bigger the better," said Lester. "A combine, a swatter, and a tractor to pull them."

Lundeen's eyebrows raised. "How much land do you farm?" he asked.

"A section," was Lester's answer.

"It'll hardly pay to have that much machinery, will it?" queried Lundeen.

"I'll hire out, and pay for it in a year," was Lester's reply. "Next year I'll double the acreage."

"Will your mother go along with that big a loan?" Lundeen asked.

"Probably not, and I don't intend to ask her. This is my idea, not hers—" he added, "If you'll trust me."

Lundeen stood, extended his hand, "Come back with some facts and figures" he said.

Lester smiled, "That's exactly what Mama said the first time I asked her for help."

Harris Brothers was the biggest farm implement agency in town. The younger Harris saw Lester looking at the machines on display, introduced himself, and recognized the name when Lester responded.

"You're looking to modernize?" he asked. Lester only nodded. "Here's a John Deere with a power-takeoff. You want to start small?"

Lester shrugged, "Actually, no. That International Harvester," he pointed, "Is that the biggest one?"

"Yeah, and it matches with the swatter and the pick-up," said Harris. Lester asked, "Will a big Farmall pull it?" Again Harris agreed.

A swatter is really named for the swath it cuts, which can be twenty feet wide, even more. Conveyers work from both ends to bring the cut grain to a winrow in the center. Thus, a large swath could be picked up by the combine and threshed. A pick-up is an attachment that conveys the swathed winrow into the belly of the combine where threshing reduces it to grain and straw. The grain is elevated to a hopper and the straw is blown out the back.

When Lester and young Harris finished figuring, the first question was, "Can you go that high?"

"I don't know, but I'll be back."

Lundeen looked at the figures, "That's a lot of debt to start with. One bad year, you could lose your shirt."

"When my grandfather Lohmann came to you for money, he came with the same risks, right? I give you my hand and my word. Your loan will be paid with interest in a year, two at the most."

Lundeen turned to the phone and called Harris, "Young Sorby is here to borrow for his machinery. I think he's a good risk; I'm loaning him the full amount." He turned to Lester, hand extended, "Your hand and your word, young man. You're a chip off the old block."

When Mina saw the machinery trundling into the yard, her reaction to Lester was, "How are we ever going to pay for all this?"

All Lester said was, "This is not 'we,' Mama. I borrowed the money. I'll pay it back."

For the coming harvest, Lester signed up for half what a threshing crew would cost. He hired two neighbor boys, the Olson brothers: one to drive the tractor and one to haul grain. Lester sat atop the combine and operated it. With headlights on the tractor, they worked long hours into the night. They stripped farms of their harvest and moved on. When it rained, they serviced their machinery. When the harvest was over, Lester had combined thousands of acres. The Olson boys were well paid, and Lester took full payment to the bank. In proving himself, Lester became something of a hero. When Lester went to Harris Brothers for parts replacement, he found that they were taking orders for next year's harvest machinery.

The elder Harris smiled, "You started something, young man."

Lester turned twenty-one in the fall. He still read only one magazine, "The Successful Farmer." Now with confidence he felt that he too had earned the title. Also he was seeing more of Maybelle. She was struggling with the older boys in her one-room school. Lester, both anxious and worried, found himself in a relationship dictated by instinct. Maybelle was finding an escape from the school house.

Mina watched and wondered. "She's no wife for a farmer," she thought. In the busy time of spring seeding she sat down with Lester. They talked about the land that he was renting, another whole section to the west. She asked him what he planned to seed. It was to be his land, his profit or loss. When they finished, Lester said, "Another thing, Mama, Maybelle and I are getting married."

Mina held her tongue as Lester went on.

"She can take over a lot of the work you do. She'll be a big help."

Mina bowed her head, "She'll take over all right, Lester. You're a farmer, a good one, but she won't ever be a good farmer's wife."

Lester, jaw set, stubborn, torn between the two women in his life, said, "We have to. She's expecting."

Eye to eye they sat. "That too," said Mina. She paused, "Marrying Jacob, your father, meant a lot of hard work and little else. You're a worker, Lester, always have been. I want you to have it as good as you can. You and Honus and this farm are all I have."

"Maybelle wants to live here. She wants to help; she wants you to have a grandchild," Lester said.

"What she wants is you, Lester. She's already got what she wants."

Lester and Maybelle were married before the Justice of the Peace. Maybelle left her school. The school board didn't want a married teacher, let alone a pregnant one. She moved into Lester's bedroom, slept late in the mornings and watched an uncomplaining Mina run her house. In the late summer before the baby came, she seldom left her room. Evenings after the long working days of harvest, Mina would see Lester carrying a slop jar from their bedroom to empty it outside. Mina's torment deepened when the baby came; a small deformed creature that screamed in high-pitched agony instead of crying. Lester was aging almost overnight. His success in farming barely outweighed his emotional defeat at home.

The baby died before snowfall. A grieving Lester buried her beside her grandfather. There would be no more children.

When Mina and Lester sat down to settle accounts for the year, Mina told him it was time she turned the farm over to him. They would share equally from the home farm. Lester could rent and harvest as he saw fit.

"This will be Maybelle's house. There isn't room for two women," she said.

A troubled Lester asked, "Where would you go?"

"I don't know just yet," she said. "Honus doesn't belong here; he never will. I don't think either one of us belongs here now."

In November, Mina and Honus said goodbye to a very self-satisfied Maybelle, and Lester drove them to town.

Still wondering, Lester asked her. "Where to, Mama?"

"The Greyhound bus station," Mina replied. "We're going to California."

EPILOGUE

Lester and Honus were close in ways that defy understanding. Both had grown up fatherless, but fatherless in far different ways. Lester had watched in terror and panic as Jacob was shot by Uncle Frank. He never mentioned it ever in the years that followed. Honus never thought of anyone as father. The man who had sired him had been referred to as Ted. That was really all he knew. When the minister said he was a nameless person his identity was frozen in place. Lester grew up never wanting to be a child. He spent his adult life pursuing childhood through the lives of others, never through his own. Honus, the child, had the instincts of a man, always rejecting the man who had caused him.

Lester didn't really walk, he shambled. As a small boy Honus would follow him and try to imitate his bowlegged, pigeon-toed gait. At that, everyone smiled, even Lester. When Lester would stand arms akimbo staring toward the horizon, the small shadow behind him would also. The word love was never spoken in the household. It was acted out, never spoken.

Edwards Brothers, Inc.
Thorofare, NJ USA
November 29, 2011